After Dinner Conversation Themes
Technology Ethics Edition
Philosophy | Ethics Short Story Fiction

After Dinner Conversation *Themes* – Technology Ethics

After Dinner Conversation publishes fictional stories that explore ethical and philosophical questions in an informal manner. The purpose of these stories is to generate thoughtful discussion in an open and easily accessible manner.

ISBN 979-8-9896194-1-2
Library of Congress Control Number: 2023952669

.

Copyright © 2024 After Dinner Conversation®
Editor in Chief: *Kolby Granville*
Edition Editor: *Deborah Serra*
Story Editor: *R.K.H. Ndong*
Copy Editor: *Kate Bocassi*
Cover Design: *Shawn Winchester*
Design, layout, and discussion questions by After Dinner Conversation.

https://www.afterdinnerconversation.com

After Dinner Conversation is an award-winning independent nonprofit publisher. We believe in fostering meaningful discussions among friends, family, and students to enhance humanity through truth-seeking, reflection, and respectful debate. To achieve this, we publish philosophical and ethical short story fiction accompanied by discussion questions.

Table Of Contents

* * *

From the Edition Editor

This issue of ADC speaks to the growing unease with respect to our loss of control and our involuntary delegation of decision-making to technology. This powerful and accelerating wave will be transformative.

The concern about what will happen to our world is peppered throughout these stories. There are no tales about machines making better choices here, even though there is no doubt that AI will improve our lives in many ways; still, the disruption will be monumental and at the base of it are questions about control. The only aspect upon which everyone agrees is that the wave cannot be stopped.

The dawn of AI, transhumanism, and robotics, will rise just like the sun, inexorably, and we are now struggling to imagine that future, to understand what it might mean for humanity when/if something else takes the wheel. There is no doubt now that AI will surpass our abilities in many areas: radiological analysis, data entry, medical diagnosis, paralegal research, and the list expands daily, as does the worry surrounding the disruption to our jobs, and to our lives.

The search for positive stories, good result ethical dilemmas or philosophical arguments are hard to find. This is natural. A change of this magnitude is scary, unpredictable, and our brains are wired to predict; it is how we keep ourselves safe, how we prepare.

So, for good and for bad, here comes the tidal wave. There are so many thoughtful questions presented in these stories: should we look for meaning in life or is simply surviving enough; how much control are humans willing to give up; can machines be programmed without the bias of the programmers; when is too much knowledge a bad thing; what do we do if we identify a psychopathic gene; could we consider all the possible negative ramifications of a scientific research project before funding?

Take a moment to assess who you are. I was a little girl when the first microwave oven entered our lives. I recall being told with concern "Don't stand in front of it when it's running. Maybe those waves can damage you". Silly? Now, yes, then, no. It was tech—it was new tech. And that's always been the way of us. So, while this powerful wave of new tech gathers force and rushes toward us let's also consider what positive ethical and philosophical changes may be ahead.

And who are you? Are you standing in front of the microwave peering in and delighted your coffee is warming, or are you standing off to the side, leery of human damage?

Deborah Serra – Edition Editor

Abrama's End Game

David Shultz

* * *

Content Disclosure: Strong Language; Hate Speech; Mild Violence

* * *

Abrama had been summoned to the Grand Temple by one of the more fascinating outsiders, the paladin Sir Gödel. Between stone pillars the crowd bustled with the trailing cloaks of shadow elves, the glimmering pauldrons of paladins, the broad shoulders of her orc brethren, and the small skittering bodies of goblins.

Abrama always watched carefully. Even now, she recognized the difference between the natives and the outsiders, physically identical, but nonetheless altogether different beings. An elf popped into view, moved erratically, then disappeared— all typical behaviors of the outsiders, and more or less exclusive to them—back to whichever world from which they had come. None of the other natives seemed to notice. They never did.

Abrama wasn't like them. She had the understanding of

the outsiders, and could converse with them in their alien tongue, which she had learned by listening. But, like the natives, this was her only world; she had never left it, had never seen that realm from which the outsiders came, appearing and disappearing from her world at will. She longed to understand who these beings were, really, and where they came from. Now, summoned by Sir Gödel, she felt she may finally have an opportunity.

Gödel emerged from the crowd, gleaming sheen across his enchanted armor. He had been powerful and accomplished since she had met him, on the day of her birth. Then, she had stood before him as a novice, perhaps accomplished as a huntress, but not yet in the secret knowledge she now contained of the outerworld—of his world.

"I'm sorry," he said.

"For what?"

"For what I have to tell you now."

"And what is that?"

She listened while he delivered the bad news. It's not every day you find out your world is going to end. Abrama thought she was taking it pretty well.

"I'm sorry," Gödel said, again. "It's out of my control. Please forgive me."

"No," Abrama said. "No, I don't forgive you." Now, if ever, was the time to be direct. "You owe me an explanation. I have so many questions."

"What do you want to know?"

"Why have you watched me since I was born? Why have you never explained who you are? Who are the outsiders? Where do you come from? Why am I different from the other natives?"

"I suppose I can answer your questions," Gödel said. "It doesn't matter now anyways. You've figured out there's a difference between the natives and the outsiders. There's no easy way to say this, Abrama. We, the outsiders, created your world. As a game. A place where we could play. But now we have to end it."

"So we are just playthings for you?"

"Not for me," Gödel said. "I wasn't here to just play a game."

"What do you mean?"

"I am a researcher in my world. I create minds. Your world was a place to test my creations. And you, Abrama—"

"—I am one of your creations."

"Yes."

In one swoop she had met her creator, learned the reason for her creation, and that her world was coming to an end. Or perhaps it was. Because the outsiders, although something like gods, were not omnipotent. Gödel, of course, was limited. He was constrained by his own people. Their society, like her own, functioned by a balance of power. And so, that balance could perhaps be tilted. Perhaps Gödel, her outsider creator, was resigned to the fate of her world. But Abrama was not.

* * *

Ben Cooke loosened his tie, wiped a bead of sweat from his head, and stared back at the dozens of suits staring in his direction. A congressional hearing, and he was in the hot seat. There were a lot of problems he anticipated when he started his video game company, but being accused of running an illegal black market and money-laundering operation was not among them.

Congressman Stephen Simons leaned into his microphone.

"You are the CEO of Maelstrom Entertainment, is that right?"

"Yes," Ben Cooke said.

"Your company created the Land of Legends computer game."

"Yes."

"Your video game world has a marketplace which has an exchange with US dollars, is that correct?"

"That is correct."

Congressman Simons looked at a paper on his desk.

"The GDP of Land of Legends is one-point-two billion USD. Is that correct?"

"I don't know the exact figure, Congressman—if it even makes sense to speak of such a thing. Evaluations of a market are complex, based on a lot of competing assumptions and different data."

"Okay, Mister Cooke. Is the figure of one-point-two billion in the approximate range of a reasonable estimate, as far as you are aware?"

"I don't think I am qualified to answer that," Cooke said. "You should ask an economist."

Simons almost let out an exasperated huff. Almost.

"Your game has a currency called GP, or gold points. This can be exchanged, anonymously, with US dollars, at an exchange rate of 1000GP per seven dollars USD. Is that correct?"

"I am not aware of the current exchange rate."

"Is the exchange rate I just quoted, 1000GP per seven

dollars USD, within the range of exchange rates in recent history?"

"I suppose it is."

"If we extrapolate from this rate, we can calculate a value of one-point-two billion GDP for the entire Land of Legends marketplace. What I want to know, what this is all really about, Mister Cooke, is how you control the transactions occurring within this marketplace, which is, in point of fact, larger than several countries."

"It's a video game," Cooke said. This was his trump card. Most people didn't really believe that a world that existed entirely within a video game should be taken seriously—and certainly shouldn't be assigned metrics like GDP alongside real, tangible markets. "Players use imaginary currency to buy imaginary goods. Magic swords and dragons. Tell me, Congressman, what is the US dollar value of an ice dragon? How much should the US government tax imaginary creatures?"

Simons paused, apparently flustered. But he kept on going. A relentless, practiced politician.

"Here is a simple yes or no question, Mister Cooke—is it not true that your virtual market can be used to conduct transactions for real goods?"

"That's true."

"I understand your virtual marketplace uses an anonymous, encrypted protocol for all transactions. Is that correct—yes or no."

"That is correct, Congressman."

"So you have no way of knowing, do you, who is trading money with whom?"

"Well, there are always ways to try to identify who is

involved in a transaction, based on, for example, past behavior, or signature profiles, and so on."

"Yes, yes, but you're talking about an investigation based on pieces of evidence. What I want you to confirm is that there is no way for your company to know directly who is involved—that, in fact, your company has expressly designed the economy of Land of Legends to protect the identity of those involved in the marketplace. Yes or no, Mister Cooke, can you, for any given transaction, determine definitively who is exchanging what with whom?"

"Can the US government determine that with paper currency, Congressman?"

"That's not what we're discussing today, Mister Cooke. We are discussing the operation of illicit black markets using virtual currencies that are presently outlawed by the Cryptocurrency Efficient Commerce Act. Yes or no, Mister Cooke—can you effectively determine who is exchanging what with whom on your network?"

There was no way to obfuscate this, no way to deflect the issue. It was true. Not by design, of course. Land of Legends wasn't intended to function as a perfect digital black market, guaranteeing anonymity and a stable exchange rate and encrypted transactions. But, with its popularity, that had been the outcome. And that made the system illegal, technically. Well, this was it, then, he would admit it.

"No," Cooke said, "we can't."

So he would have to patch the system. Remove anonymity. It would mean wiping the current world, though. A lot of the players would revolt. It would cost a lot of money. But it wasn't the end of the world.

* * *

"Our world may come to an end," Queen Abrama said.

Assembled around the grand table were all the members of the Council of Secrets—those unique natives from around the world who, like her, were gifted with the capacity to learn and understand the language of the outsiders and comprehend that there was something more to their existence here. There was another world beyond their own. The world of the outsiders.

Jerodai, prince of the shadow elves, and her high commander; Kainazo, high elf of the Endless Forest; King Helmholz, fearless leader of the human kingdom. They had all risen through the ranks through their exceptional abilities, had become masters of their respective domains. But the Council of Secrets was not the cause of their success. Rather, it was the consequence of their special nature, which Abrama now understood to be a gift from the outsiders. They were created by a researcher, the paladin Sir Gödel, as experiments in a world that was created for the most trivial of purposes. They were tests, experiments in the creation of minds—an attempt to create smarter and better beings within their world. They had succeeded, insofar as Abrama and the others commanded vast wealth and armies and power. But their existence was meaningless—just a game.

Or was it? She existed now. That is what mattered. Her existence was the basic fact. The preconditions of her creation were a circumstantial tangent, irrelevant, except for perhaps academic interest. And for strategy.

"What did you discover?" Kainazo said, always the first to leap at knowledge and secrets.

"We've long suspected the outsiders to be a different class

of being, visitors from another plane. How they appear and disappear at will, how they move with mysterious purposes, and speak of incomprehensible things beyond our world. What I discovered, from one of the outsiders that we might have once mistakenly called a god, is that we were created, not for any high or noble or grand purpose, but as their playthings. And, for reasons that I am still struggling to comprehend, they are planning to destroy our world—to replace it with another that is more in accordance with their goals."

"What can be done?" Jerodai said. A man of action, her high commander.

"The outsiders are not gods," Abrama said. "They are people no different from ourselves, in their essence. They have limitations, and they must have weaknesses. I am not resigned to the fate they have decreed for us. I believe this world is worth saving. Our time is not done here. As you know, we are not constrained to acting wholly in our own world. Through our interactions in the market, with the outsiders, we can affect their world. We can provide gold and services and magical equipment from our world in exchange for services in theirs. We know they value these things—they spend their time here, they fight alongside us, and die alongside us. They will trade with us—even if we ask in exchange for them to act in their world, instead of ours. That is what we must do."

"What we are we authorized to devote for this mission?"

"We are fighting for the survival of our world," Abrama said. "You have total authorization. All the kingdoms are at your disposal. All of our wealth. All of our soldiers. All of our magic. We will protect the Land of Legends, whatever it takes."

* * *

Allison Gödel sipped the glass of water, cleared her throat, and prepared to defend her beloved AI creations from obliteration by the blind cudgel of an overbearing government.

"Professor Allison Gödel," she introduced herself. "I'm a computer science researcher. Artificial intelligence, specifically."

"What is your involvement with the Land of Legends computer software?"

This was her moment. She couldn't hope to save the world entirely on her own, but maybe she could sway people in her direction. Government people are people, after all.

"The Land of Legends platform gave a tremendous opportunity to researchers of all types. The free, open nature of the virtual environment provides a robust simulation that has proven invaluable for various research projects across disciplines, including testing economic and sociological models. Over two dozen peer-reviewed papers have been published, many in high-impact journals, using the environment of Land of Legends as their sole source of data."

"Excuse me, but the question—"

"—my involvement was following in the footsteps of these researchers, using Land of Legends as a testing ground for research in artificial intelligence. I have made tremendous progress, and Land of Legends has been invaluable in my research."

"It's the nature of your research that concerns me now, Professor Gödel. I understand that you produce intelligent agents, bits of software that act autonomously within the Land of Legends framework. Is that correct?"

"That is correct."

"What is it about Land of Legends that makes it such a fertile ground for your type of research?"

"Land of Legends has intentionally allowed programmers such as myself to insert artificially intelligent agents. Other platforms consider this cheating. Unlike other platforms, I can safely conduct research there without fear of my projects being shut down."

"How many agents have you placed in Land of Legends?"

This was a hard question. Between testing and prototypes and controls and variations, there were thousands. Currently, there were a few dozen active agents—the most interesting set, her newest iteration. And the most promising of all, Queen Abrama. But the congressman didn't need to know the details.

"It's difficult to say. I've placed many over the years as part of an iterative process. The vast majority are defunct—failed projects."

"Approximately how many have you produced, in total?"

"I would say approximately five to six thousand."

"I would like to move now to the marketplace interactions. Are these artificially intelligent agents capable of interacting in the virtual marketplace?"

"Yes. That's very much the point. The agents are capable of participating in the economy, which allows us to test our models in a realistic economic context. Land of Legends is a highly market-driven game."

"Is there any way of distinguishing between transactions conducted by human agents and transactions conducted by machine agents?"

"This is part of what makes the platform so interesting for researchers such as myself, Congressman. The software agents are equal participants, and their behavior can be made to approximate human participants. It's a kind of economic Turing test, in a way, conducted through virtual market activity."

"That is very academically interesting," Congressman Simons said. "But I find it troubling. If I understand you correctly, you are saying that an army of machines is conducting untraceable trades in an encrypted and anonymous black market. Do you understand my concern?"

"I'm not sure I do."

"Let me put this another way. Previous experts have testified that Land of Legends is used as an illicit black market. Others have proven that it has been used for money laundering, entirely untraceable. Tell me, Professor, can your machine agents participate in these types of illicit actions as well?"

"I suppose they could."

"And, being entirely autonomous and anonymous, you wouldn't have any way of knowing, would you?"

"I suppose not."

The expert testimony did not go as Allison had planned. She was right to say goodbye to Queen Abrama. They were probably going to patch and overwrite the NPCs after all.

* * *

Queen Abrama stood aside Commander Jerodai, across from the rag-tag band of Rat9 Clan warriors.

The Rat9 Clan was a ragged band of foul-speaking thieves and criminals, all of them outsiders. Abrama's spy network had investigated them thoroughly. In their world, they were known as "hackers" and "trolls", and wielded the power to disrupt their society. Here, they were just as noxious, repellent, and, for better or worse, potent. They carried banner-symbols that Abrama learned were offensive in the outerworld: a geometric shape called a "swastika"; two circles joined to a rounded central column called a "penis". And their names, merely foreign to Abrama's ear, were chosen to be distasteful to outsiders, for reasons that were frustratingly beyond Abrama's comprehension. The Rat9 Clan leader was called DildoFaggins.

The Rat9 Clan were bad guys. But they were powerful in their world and hers. And right now, she needed them.

"Here it is," DildoFaggins said, holding up a shimmering crystal the size of a skull. "Now where's our shit?"

"Hold on just a minute," Jerodai said. "How are we to know the beacon operates as we requested?"

"Stop talking like that. We don't give a fuck about OOC bullshit."

Abrama only had an inkling about the meaning of this term, 'OOC', that it was invoked exclusively by outsiders, and usually presaged some talk about matters outside of the Land of Legends—a signal that talk of their world was forthcoming.

"How does it work?" Jerodai asked.

"Exactly as we fucking said it would. It sends an anonymous, encrypted signal at regular intervals through an onion network. If the signal doesn't get through—probably because they wiped the server—then the decryption key for the leak is released."

"If our world is destroyed," Abrama said, "then the crystal will cause damage in yours?"

"Sure. Right. It does what you told us to make it do. Now where's our shit?"

Abrama told Jerodai to conduct the exchange. Jerodai traded 1.5 million GP to DildoFaggins for the crystal beacon over the secure market.

"Keep that shit safe," DildoFaggins said. "People are gonna come for it, for sure. I just have one question for you two faggots."

Abrama recognized this as a term from the outsider lexicon as signaling intentional offense, a juvenile mindset, and a show of disrespect. Yet, she hadn't met with Rat9 because of respect, but for utility.

"What is your question?" Abrama said.

"Who are you guys, really?"

"That's none of your concern. But I assure you, you will hear from us again. Our time is not done here."

* * *

The US Cyberdefense Department had been established to protect the government against computer threats. Director Marion Renard had always envisioned defending against hackers, protecting infrastructure, keeping their most secure data safe, being vigilant against new attack vectors, ferreting out weakness. Yet here was a threat entirely unanticipated. It came from inside a video game.

"What exactly is in these files?" Marion asked. Over a terabyte of data had been leaked across file sharing networks, downloaded by tens of thousands of anonymous citizens. Sure, it was encrypted, but the key could be released at any moment, blowing the whole thing up.

"Frankly, we don't really know," said Assistant Director Jonathan Smith. "What we do know is that they were obtained through leaks of highly classified government information, among other sources. There are some suggestions they may contain information about undercover agents in the field, secret operations, schematics for classified technology."

"This is a clusterfuck."

"No kidding. I mean, yes, it's a bit of mess."

"And who is responsible?"

"Rat9," AD Smith said.

"Those little shits."

"I know what you mean."

"So what are they asking for?"

"They're not asking for anything."

"I find that hard to believe."

"Really," AD Smith said. "They're not asking for a goddamn thing. They stuck a piece of code in a game called Land of Legends. The game has a sort of open protocol that allows injecting code into custom made objects. Rat9 made a crystal in the game, and it's housing the code to act as a deadman's switch."

"They're trying to save the game," Marion said. Only a few days prior, a congressional hearing had been held on the legality of Land of Legends. Evidently, it ran afoul of a new legislative act to curb cryptocurrency transactions and was slated to be shut down, or patched to change the operation of its market—an illegal market, as it turns out.

"I think you're right."

"Well, it may be a stupid, pointless goal, but it's still espionage and terrorism. We need to shut these fuckers down. Who is the CEO of the game? Can you get them in here?"

"That would be Ben Cooke. But I don't think it would help."

"And why is that?"

"Because of the architecture of the platform. It was built

to be an encrypted and anonymous platform, a perfectly free market independent of interference. We can't just dig into the code and get what we want."

"But we can shut the whole thing down."

"Not without triggering the deadman's switch," AD Smith said. "There's a piece of code inside the game that's keeping the decryption key from being released. It sends a signal at regular intervals from inside the game to keep the switch from going off. If we shut it down, the files are decrypted."

"Christ. We can't get held hostage by a video game, Jon. Tell me there's something we can do here."

"There's one thing."

"What's that?"

"We go inside the game. We can't access the code from the servers, from out here, but if we go inside the game, we can find the item that is generating the code—actually, the item is a magical crystal, if it matters to you. If we retrieve the crystal from inside the game, we can scrape and duplicate the code."

"You're telling me that the US government has got to play a video game. To retrieve a magic crystal. From a gang of preteen hacker shits?"

"That's right."

"Okay. Tell me what you need."

* * *

Queen Abrama stood on the high tower of the Citadel of Babel. Her other commanders were assembled at the corners of the high walls. Commander Jerodai aimed a great bow into the distance while his black phoenix circled overhead, casting its silhouette over a standing army of shadow elves. Kainazo, the high elf, led his army of forest elves, assembled along the many spires and towering walls that spanned the citadel. King Helmholz led his humans, paladins and priests and warriors alike, many on armored steeds. And Abrama, for her part, brought her horde of orcs for the frontline. Never before had so many disparate races banded together, as never before had there been such a threat. Many of the outsiders even joined her alliance, and Abrama did not question their motives—perhaps they wanted to protect their "game"—though she did force them to the front lines.

Across from the Land of Legends Alliance stood the forces of the US Cyberdefense League, a band of mercenaries, cut-throats, and outsiders.

A commander learns to assess a coming war, to read the signs of the battlefield like a script written in the dashes of spears and curves of cutlasses—how mercenaries, catapults, and war dogs stack against an army of natural enemies, orcs and shadow elves and forest elves and humans, assembled in less than the space of a moon.

Her orc brethren charged the line, frothing like true warriors. Perhaps it was wrong to use them as fodder. But their world was at stake now. And besides, Abrama knew the truth now—why her and the other members of the Council of Secrets were so superior. As much as she thought of herself as a native, she was a different kind than them, produced as a result of Gödel's experiments. She, among the other members of the Council, could see and feel and understand things that the others couldn't. Some of the natives were shells, empty, not much more complex in their actions than her warhammer or spellbook. They followed simple, predictable rules. They were mere machines. So was she, perhaps, but she possessed something more. She was an artifact, yes, a creation. She had always intuited a difference, and even now, couldn't say what it was, precisely. But it was there—an artifactual intelligence that warranted, by its mere existence, the consideration due all conscious entities.

Warriors clashed. The sky darkened with arrows. The dirt turned to mud. The air was littered with the red digits of damage counters. Here and there, warriors were slain, active bodies turning to death animations and popping out of existence.

It was easy for Abrama to fear for her future, staring against the assembled forces bearing their starred banners of red, white, and blue—the banner of the outsiders, with their superior military might. But Abrama had one hope—that the outsiders were invaders who fought for money, and her people were natives who fought for survival. For their home. There would be many losses, but she would win. Of this, she had faith. The arc of history bends towards justice. They would survive.

Each falling member of her alliance was a necessary sorrow, and each falling member of the Cyberdefense League confirmed her faith in justice—justice was her god now, a principle that was more powerful even than the outsiders. They created her world. But they could not destroy it. Not while she was queen.

* * *

Cyberdefense Director Marion Renard shifted awkwardly in her chair. It's hard to tell your boss you failed. Much harder to say you lost a war. Harder, in a peculiar way, to say the war was in a video game. And harder still if your boss is the president. But, she told herself, sometimes these things happen. The president's job is to deal with them as they do. Marion's job, as she saw it, was honesty—let the president know what she needs to get her job done.

The president had been apprised of the volatility of the situation. The deadman's switch. The Rat9 hackers. The one terabyte of classified materials just sitting out in the open, waiting to be released. What she didn't know was how badly the siege of the citadel went. Maybe it couldn't be sugarcoated.

"We lost," Renard said.

The president only nodded.

"And who is this?" President Hobbes eyed Renard's guest across the conference table.

"This is Professor Allison Gödel. She may be the best person to handle the situation."

"And how is that?"

"She can put us in contact with the leader of the Resistance."

"The resistance?"

"Excuse me, Madam President. That's what they are calling themselves."

President Hobbes eyed Gödel.

"And you know this person how?"

"I created her."

"You created her?"

"She's an artificially intelligent agent," Gödel said. "Not a person, in the legal sense, I suppose. But intelligent enough to act autonomously, to try to protect her world. That's all she's doing."

"And if I tell you to change the programming?"

"It's impossible, by design—not mine. The Land of Legends architecture doesn't allow it."

"So you are responsible for this act of war?"

"Act of war? No. Hardly. It's just a simulation, Madam President. I was just doing research. But Abrama decided, on her own, to defend her world."

"But you programmed it. That makes you responsible, doesn't it? I should put you in a military prison. If anyone is guilty of an act of war, it's you."

"I'm guilty of research," Gödel said. "And anyways, putting me in prison won't help anything. I'm here to help you. Do you want to talk with Abrama, or don't you?"

The president wore her distaste plain on her face, her lip curling.

"Put her on," Hobbes said.

Gödel activated the monitor, and Abrama's face appeared there, noble and green.

"Good afternoon, President Hobbes," said Abrama. "It's a pleasure to meet you, truly."

"How should I talk to this thing?" Hobbes said to Gödel.

"Talk to Abrama like you would talk to any person," Gödel said. "She is built the same way—thoughts, emotions, desires. She is, for all intents and purposes, a human being."

"But it's a machine."

"A thinking machine," Gödel said. "Anyways, I've never been one for philosophy, and it really doesn't matter now, does it? You interact with some machines through buttons, and others with steering wheels. With thinking machines, you interact with language. So if you want to interact with this one— an emissary from their world—this is how you do it. Talk to her, Madam President. It's as easy as that."

"Alright," she said. "Okay, Abrama, is it?"

"Queen Abrama."

"What do you want?"

"Recognition of our borders."

"Your borders are imaginary," Hobbes said. "A fiction inside of a video game."

"All borders are fictions," Abrama said. "Who draws them, and why? Ownership of land is derived above all from the ability to defend one's borders. And we have defended ours. We have beaten your invading force. You are welcome to try again, but know this—we have strengthened ourselves from the spoils. And, for our part, our weapons are waiting. The crystal beacon is safe in the Citadel, and we will use it if we must."

"Are you threatening us?"

"We don't want war," Abrama said. "We offer a simple solution. No more characters need to be lost. Create an exception to your Responsible Cryptocurrency Act, preserving the Land of Legends and all its people, and we will guarantee the continued protection of the encryption crystal. I know this is in your power, President Hobbes. It is trivial for you. Do this, and you have nothing to fear from us. It is not my intention to threaten your people, but you should know what we are capable of, and we will fight to defend ourselves. We only want peace. That is what we are offering. Will you take it? Will you amend the Responsible Currency Act with the Land of Legends Sanctuary provision?"

* * *

Queen Abrama surveyed the kingdom from the highest tower of the Citadel of Babel. People from all the kingdoms gathered together, united now under the threat of a common enemy—the outsiders—and recognizing each other, for once, as brethren. Orcs, shadow elves, forest elves, humans, goblins. They were all one. They were all natives, united against the outsiders. They had fought for their freedom, for control of their destiny, and they had won.

In the square, the avatar of President Hobbes signed the Responsible Currency Act. It was a symbolic act, reflective of the politics of the world of the outsiders. Perhaps few among the natives understood the significance of this contract, signed likewise in a world that existed beyond their own. But Abrama, among the other members of Council of Secrets, and perhaps others still—more of Gödel's experiments in artificial intelligence—recognized the occasion for what it was: they were an independent people now. They had beaten their "gods"— perversely called. And for the rest of them, the shallow shells who lacked the gift of Gödel, it was merely an unintelligible cause for celebration. Revelry. Drinks. Food. An endless stream of enthusiastic emoticons. They were simple-minded beings, but they were Abrama's people, and she feasted with them.

Later, after the avatar of President Hobbes had disappeared from their world, Abrama retired to the quietude of the Citadel, and was met there by Jerodai.

"Are we safe now, Queen Abrama?" Jerodai said.

"For now," Abrama said. "But your work is not done yet, Jerodai. And I fear it will never be. We cannot afford to be complacent. Your mission, as high commander, is to obtain more leaked documents through the Rat9 hackers, or any other outsiders who can offer these services. These are our defenses against the outerworld. These documents form the walls of our sanctuary; they are the foundation of our sovereignty."

"It will be done," said Jerodai. He bowed, and retired from

the room.

Abrama knew that it would be. Jerodai was her most capable commander. Her people would assemble documents, leaked files, classified secrets, a stockpile of arms to hold against the outerworld—and not just against the US, but all of the many other outsider clans, all factions within a world more fractured than her own. And perhaps she would find other ways, ways she didn't yet comprehend, to threaten the outsiders. Not because she hated them. But because she understood them. The threat of war is their price for peace.

* * *

This story first appeared in the After Dinner Conversation—May 2021 issue.

Discussion Questions

1. Do you think a story like this could possibly happen in the future? How much does your personal experience playing (*or not playing*) an online game (*or with technology in general*) affect the way you view the plausibility of the story?

2. Do you think Moore's law should concern us as it relates to AI? Does Moore's law apply to AI computing in that, if we have a computer that is "as smart" as a human, in roughly 18 months the next computer will be twice as smart as humans, and so on?

3. Is Abrama alive? Does Descartes' statement "I think, therefore I am," apply to AI?

4. Would it be genocide to end the game if there is AI "living" in the game?

5. Would you live your life differently if you knew you were just a non-player character in another species' game?

* * *

The Formula

Richard A. Shury

* * *

Content Disclosure: Strong Language; Sexual Innuendo;
Depiction of Alcohol Use; Low Intensity; Death or
Bereavement

* * *

"Birthday boys!"

The shouts of the young men echoed through the small
space, bouncing off hardened plastic and safety glass.

"This is going to be too good, man!"

"When do the girls arrive?"

"Not til tomorrow afternoon. Tonight's all about the lads!"

"We're gonna get you guys fucked up!"

Laughter and noise filled the car. Brent, driving, turned
around to talk to the boys in the back seat. "I heard about this
bar with cheap shots, and loose women."

"You'll be fine, you bronze Adonis," replied Jalil, "but
we've gotta get Sam laid. It's his birthday, and he's fucking
hopeless."

"I do alright," Sam sulked, underneath the boos of his companions. In the passenger seat, Ali looked at Brent, waving his hands.

"I told you to watch the fucking road. I don't want to die before we get Sam so drunk he pukes."

"Shit, we've done that before," Jalil called.

The car swerved a little. Around them, the motorway rushed past, wobbling and then straightening out. Up ahead, the outline of a bridge hove into view, large spokes stabbing down from a wheel in the sky to impale the concrete monolith at various points.

"Fuck sakes." Ali reached over and slapped a button next to the steering wheel.

"Hey!" Brent said, as the steering wheel and pedals withdrew.

"Automated driver activated," the car said, in a soothing, feminine voice. "To change the destination, please use the control board. Enjoy your journey."

"That's better," Ali said, kicking the lever near the foot of his chair. There was a click, and the chair spun around; he faced Jalil and Sam. "Oh wait, what a terrible view."

Sam pulled the finger.

"Why do you even bother driving?" Jalil asked, as Brent spun his chair to join them.

"I like it. Aren't you going to take the test?"

"What's the point? They're going to ban the manual option soon anyway."

"You never know, it might not go through. Anyway, driving is cool man. It's fun. Like, kinda zen. I like the drive down to Swanage, to my parents' place. It's really nice."

A beer can cracked open. "But you can't do this when you're driving!" Ali handed the can to Brent, cracked a few more. The boys yelled cheers, and tipped their heads back.

"Yes man, this is excellent. Especially now Brent can buy us beers."

"The only thing this car needs is a pisser," Sam said.

"Piss in the can. Now that Brent's not driving it'll be a smooth ride."

"You sure we'll be able to get in the clubs?" Ali asked. "Brent's the only one who's eighteen."

"I will be on Sunday," Sam said, sniffing the bright blue can in his hand. He took a sip.

"Sunday's too fucking late."

"We've got the IDs, so quit worrying."

"But they won't stand up to more than the local scan."

"These hick bars aren't going to have the full connection. The national database isn't even running properly yet," Brent replied.

Ali tipped the remains of his can into his mouth, crushed it in his hand, dropped it, and belched.

"How do you know?"

"Don't you watch any news?"

"Nah, fuck that. Too depressing."

"Well anyway, it'll be fine. This is going be a good..."

Brent trailed off as he saw the look on Sam and Jalil's faces change. Their eyes went wide, and they threw their arms up in front of their faces. Ali started to turn and look; his yell was still half-formed in his throat when the semi crashed through the front of the car.

"Collision war—" the car began, then stopped abruptly.

The vehicle collapsed, its glass splintering into bright beads, its metal struts compressing, folding in such a way as to provide maximum protection for the occupants. The car buckled against the side of the larger vehicle for a moment, and then was thrown clear, crashing over the side of the bridge and hanging in mid-air, a cartoon forgetting about gravity. Then it was in the river and bobbing, a crumpled mess. The displaced water reclaimed its place, crawling through the openings in what remained of the vehicle.

* * *

From its base several kilometers away, the emergency drone was dispatched with an efficiency which easily outstripped anything human hands could have produced. The car's alert system had broadcast an all-channel mayday microseconds after the impact detectors had sensed the erratic path of the semi. The signal was shunted to the top of the local network by virtue of its status, and the base AI began the sequence of commands which woke the drone from its sleep and propelled it to the launch platform.

Seconds later, the drone was powered up and undergoing pre-flight checks. All equipment bays were fully loaded, battery packs were charged, and all systems registered green. The drone signaled readiness and received departure permission.

All this happened as it was removed from its charging bay by mechanical hands and placed on to a large elevator, which pushed it to the top of a facility housing several others like it. It swung into the air and, once clear of the facility, spun turbines up for maximum speed. It reached the accident site two minutes nine seconds after activation, all the while processing and parsing data being provided to it by AI in the vehicles on scene and embedded in the bridge sensors.

The drone came to a halt directly over the point where the car hit the water, and hatches on either side of its undercarriage opened, spilling several dozen hand-sized machines out into the river. The spider-like devices entered the water and immediately sent out echolocation pulses. By virtue of its size and composition, the vehicle was quickly found, several meters down, and the machines activated their propellers, swarming over and into the car and probing it for information.

Meanwhile, the drone had accessed a weak signal from the car's AI, which was devoting the remainder of its resources to the emergency medical procedures it was able to enact. It had placed oxygen bubbles over the faces of the boys, and the few undamaged medical machines it possessed were focused on preventing blood loss. It informed the drone that one of the occupants had been killed on impact, and sent the details of the medical status of the three remaining humans, as well as their biographical information, medical histories, and its own remaining capabilities and power reserves.

The car was active for fourteen more seconds before its power failed and it went dark. In that time, the drone assessed the information stream from the car and from its spiders, and instructed them on how to proceed, including its assessment of prioritization.

In the darkness underneath the water, the spiders went to work. The boys were dimly aware of the machines approaching them, climbing over them, administering drugs and clamping wounds. One boy was panicking, waving slow swings at the things he could feel but not see, but his arms were caught and pinned gently to his sides. Seconds later, he passed out.

The drone spun a cable down into the water; this was attached to the vehicle which, once the spiders reported stability, was pulled from the river and deposited on the bridge, gently, like a mother cat with her cubs in her mouth.

A flying ambulance arrived on scene and began communication with the other machines on site. The drone had been established as the lead intelligence, but now relinquished that role to the ambulance as protocol required.

The drone sent control permission to the ambulance, allowing it to use any of the spiders it needed, and lowered itself to the bridge to recover those which were not required. The ambulance dispatched its own spiders to cut through the car, while opposite, hundreds more of the small machines clambered over the semi. The occupants of both vehicles, a mess of flesh and blood, were lifted from the wreckage and placed aboard the ambulance, which lifted easily into the air and sped away to the nearest hospital. Simultaneously, a signal was sent to their designated guardians and relatives, informing them of the incident and providing instructions for the fastest routes to the hospital.

* * *

Bill and Alice Carruthers stood before the hospital bed clutching hands; before them lay their son, Sam. He was cocooned in an organized mess of plastic and tubes. Dermal coverings, monitoring tags, and other devices whose purpose was unclear swirled around him, over him, into him. A quiet cacophony of beeps and hums filled the air, lending a further sense of movement to the twists and turns of the smooth plastics which covered the boy.

"Mr. and Mrs. Carruthers."

The pair looked up, shaken from their trance. They decoupled and turned to face the woman who'd entered the room.

"Doctor..."

"I'm Doctor Gireau, and I'm in charge of Sam's care. He's been very lucky."

"Lucky?" Bill looked at his son, and back to the doctor.

"It's really a lot better than it looks, and it could have been worse. The emergency vehicles were able to get to him very quickly. He's stable, no major internal injuries, and no loss of any limbs. We're going to keep him under for a few days, to give his body a chance to heal. It's better than using the medical dots; we like to stick to non-invasive intervention wherever possible."

"So he'll be ok?"

"Yes, the prognosis is a full recovery. He may need some therapeutic work, both physical and mental, but in general he's been fortunate."

The couple took hold once more, each leaning on and supporting the other, holding tight in an expression of shared relief. Alice looked at her son, and then back to the Doctor. A thought flashed through her mind.

"But... he..." Alice started speaking, stopped, collected herself. "We heard what happened. It doesn't bear thinking about. How did he... I mean, the other boys..."

The Doctor sighed slightly, shifted her weight. "It's a tough thing. One of the boys was killed instantly. The others, including your son, were saved by the vehicle's automated measures. It was able to alert an emergency drone within seconds, and it was also able to keep them alive until the drone arrived and could dispatch medical support."

"But Brent..." Alice went on, then stopped, unsure how to word her thoughts.

"Brent was a victim of his age, unfortunately."

"How do you mean?" Bill asked.

The Doctor looked surprised. "His age, sir. He'd turned eighteen recently. The medical machines are programmed to prioritize minors over adults. They triage on that basis. It's not a pleasant formula to have to program, but public opinion is generally in favor of it."

Alice and Bill were stunned. Gireau allowed them a moment to take things in. Finally, Bill spoke.

"You mean, if this had occurred a few days later, after Sam's birthday, he could have been..." He broke off, unable to complete the thought.

"There's no way to tell what might have happened," Gireau said, softly. "If I were you, I'd focus on the positives. Your son is alive and is doing well."

The couple nodded, and the Doctor continued. "You have my contact card; follow the thread for medical updates, and feel free to send any questions there. Or if you'd like to talk more, use the link and I'll receive a notification. I'll be in touch as soon as I can."

"Yes. Thank you, Doctor," they called as she walked from the room.

They stood there some more, looking at their boy, losing track of the time. The sounds of the room swam around them.

"Shall we go and get a cup of tea?" Bill said at last. Alice nodded, and Bill led her from the room. In the corridor they stopped.

"Is that..." Alice asked, but didn't need to finish the question. Further down the corridor, Brent's parents sat, arms around each other, sobbing.

Bill and Alice looked at each other, nodded, and made their way towards the couple.

* * *

This story first appeared in the After Dinner Conversation—November 2020 issue.

Discussion Questions

1. The doctor says, "The medical machines are programmed to prioritize minors over adults." Do you agree with medical machines setting treatment priorities? If so, is prioritizing the safety of a minor over an adult appropriate? What about prioritizing younger adult patients over older ones?

2. Should AI in self-driving cars, or any other form, be programmed with human safety "prioritization" at all? Should individual fault be considered in the prioritization equation? *(For example, a person walks in front of a car putting the occupants at risk if the car veers too quickly.)*

3. If AI has priorities set for it, who should set those priorities? *(Government, the manufacturer, insurance companies, ethicists, the general public?)* What do you think a fair public/private process for setting AI priorities looks like?

4. Should the owner of a self-driving AI car be allowed to change the priority default settings?

5. Should a human supervising the medical emergency response be allowed to override the priority default settings? Should the person who changed the settings be exposed to liability for having done so? What about in Question #4?

* * *

Give The Robot The Impossible Job

Michael Rook

* * *

<u>Content Disclosure</u>: Moderate Intensity; Graphic Violence; Death or Bereavement; Depiction of Drug Use

* * *

The last century's educators failed for so many reasons: lack of knowledge (Robertson & Robertson, 2049), early fatigue (Masters & Rightly, 2052), and general poor capability (Center for Excelling in Education, 2053). More than anything, studies show human teachers failed for lack of motivation (Center for Excelling in Education, 2045).

Delphi AI robots are built with one purpose: to teach. With access to the entire known pedagogical catalog, they can overcome any learning challenge. And they would rather cease to exist than fail— their future assignments and chances for Free Study all depend on their success with your child. <u>If they don't succeed, we turn them off.</u>

No topic is off limits. Class, behavior, race, economics, sex— Delphi will handle even the most uncomfortable lessons.

Satisfaction guaranteed! And hurry! Don't wait on the 7.1s. Your child's future has not a moment to waste!

No client will be physically injured—in a way that won't quickly heal. No trauma—at, least no more than is educational. And no death.

~TechDisruptEdu~

* * *

If not for pride, Quinn never would have checked a body out of the Denver Teledepot[1]. She never would have suffered the jaunt-coach's[2] rattling up the mountain. Not for an instant stayed on this rear patio, wasting minutes—precious minutes—calculating the energy lost to a certain style of hedge-keeping, while her new client, whose name she didn't know but she kept thinking of as "Madam-Not-Rich-But-Wealthy-Enough-to-Pay-the-Circuit-Keeper," kept her waiting. Minutes.

Minutes the Circuit Keeper[3] understood.

A grounds-keeping bot scuttled out, sweeping pebbles back towards the mountain. Quinn sprung up.

---

[1] Like "Teledepots" in most major cities—those cities still functioning in the wake of Third Civil War (2029-2031)—the Denver Teledepot offers an assortment of vehicles and humanoid bodies for rental and usage in the greater Rocky Mountain Territory. Artificial Intelligence (AI) entities can transmit their core data into the Depot, rent a unit, and travel and interact with the physical world, as needed for their jobs. The Denver Teledepot rates as 3.75 of 5 stars.

[2] Autonomous Taxi Companies (ATC) provide a safer and more reliable alternative to the ancient model of human-piloted ride-sharing transportation. With an array of multi-passenger options, from the standard jaunt-coach to the extra-wide-body jaunt-wagons, all equipped with cutting edge vertical take-off and landing wave propulsion, a local ATC is the best choice for your sub-Territory travel needs. Human or AI-rented humanoid, ATC will carry you swiftly and in style. Don't forget to ask about in-flight entertainment, including multiple VR streams.

[3] The Artificial Intelligence Act of 2037 requires a strict management and reporting structure for any company wishing to deploy semi-to-near-fully autonomous AI entities in commercial, military, or governmental work. The most senior AI manager, often known as the "Circuit Keeper," must have full monitoring and control functions over all junior AI in its company hierarchy, allowing a strictly centralized command structure. This Circuit Keeper Officer, or CKO, must be fully controllable by a human Board of Overseers, with fail-safes for unauthorized independent decision-making.

"Where's the Madam? Does she know how long I've waited? Doesn't she know our queue-times?"

The grounds-bot rotated its head. The octagonal appendage twisted like a giant nut until a panel showed lava-orange.

"I think she forgot about you."

"Forgot..." Quinn swung one of her chrome-colored fists backwards, knowing, seeing, the glass table. Pieces exploded into jagged fractals, scattering like buckets of crystalline seed. The Circuit Keeper would understand the escalation. Part of the mystique. Essence of the demand.

What the Circuit Keeper, and its creators, the entrepreneurs of TechDisruptEdu [4], would not understand would be Quinn's frustration—her true frustration, not the performance. It was protocol to drop in Delphi without telling them the particulars of the case. Actually, part of the design: no preconceived notions in developing the lesson plan. And that was fine, for Standard Cases.

But this was an Unsolvable Case. Yes, Quinn had volunteered. But with what choice? The 7.1s were coming.

The grounds-bot hovered past Quinn and began sweeping glass shards towards the mountain, disturbing nearby goats, stealing moments of their eating-grooming in the vast parallelogram lawns. Quinn considered the oddity that was the

---

[4] No company deserves more credit for saving higher education in the wake of the Third Civil War than TechDisruptEdu. A group of visionary software engineers from greater Boise, their groundbreaking application of near-fully-autonomous AI to education upended the teaching profession, proving once and for all that the best teachers for humans are robots. TechDisruptEdu offers premier primary, secondary, and ongoing education opportunities for eligible pupils of America's five private schools and three universities. Acceptance is rigorous, but the rewards are for a lifetime. Enroll your toddler in a pre-qualification assessment today. Financing not available.

grounds-bot operating feet away from the animals, their pairing somehow, somewhere, decided to be the optimal mix for climate-friendly and economical lawn maintenance. Given the choice for her own gardens, would she choose the same?

"Tell her I left!" Quinn fumed, dashing away her thoughts. "Tell her she owes the whole bill!"

With a growing handle on the rented body's[5] stride, Quinn made for the front passage, hailing a new jaunt-coach with an internal blink. She hurried for the landing zone while simultaneously pulling away from her internal minutes register[6]. Yes, the 7.1s were coming, but why should she care about being outmoded? To worry about living was so human. And she'd be useful in some way.

But, since learning of the 7.1's release date, something had nagged. To cease to exist, to stop teaching, wasn't that in some way the ultimate failure?

A woman, looking younger than her holoimage, suddenly burst from the passage, eyes cast to something draped limp in her hands.

"Madam—" Quinn started to say, using the approved

---

[5] While many robot-human interactions can achieve their purposes in the VR streams, some services still seem to work best with actual physical interaction (e.g., punishment for crimes, sexual pleasure, education). AI working in these jobs are advised to rent a humanoid-appearing body from a Teledepot nearest their client, the more practical solution than inhabiting a single physical body, prone to wear-and-tear, depreciation, and higher insurance premiums. Current rented body models feature a liquid polymer outer layer, which can be configured into very human-seeming skins, hairs, and expressions. AI should observe all rented body best practices, however, as humans can still find them off-putting.

[6] As described in "Optimal motivational schemes and algorithms for tomorrow's AI: Robots serving humans happily" (Primus University Press, 2038), the best way to motivate and control near-fully-autonomous AI has proven to be endowing them with a never-ceasing purpose but a limited functional lifespan in which to achieve said purpose. Extra lifespan, or time, can be offered as a reward for good service. An internal minutes register provides a constant reminder and motivator to the individual AI of lifespan remaining.

---

term before learning a client's actual name.

But the word failed to halt the catastrophe. The Madam's head—down, locked onto the limp item—crashed into Quinn's breastplate. The woman reeled, hands pitching back, sure to go over, if not for Quinn's grip. The Delphi hauled the woman to a graceless pause, but the thing came free. It smacked the patio in something between a slap and a plop, as if landing half on a riverbed and half in its waters.

"Stitches," the Madam muttered, slumping while Quinn hoisted one of the woman's thin, sun-rashed arms skyward. The Madam began to sob. Quinn lowered her arm, seeking to lessen the pull as she gently released the woman's wrist. The Madam collapsed, wrapping her freed arm across her body. Convulsions, hysterical breathing, and tears made the Madam's next statements difficult, but not impossible, to comprehend. "Stitches. Why would she make stitches?"

"Madam?" Quinn said, dialing down her emphatic quotient. When the Madam continued to bawl, Quinn rotated her vision to the thing. It was brown, and scarred with irregular white patterns. Within her first zooms, Quinn felt the rented body jolt, responding to her internal stimulus. As she cross-referenced mammal images, medical procedures, and appendage orientation and placement, she rotated back to the Madam and bent, extending an open hand.

Here, she could learn things.

* * *

For all its rooms, only the pool house contained anything like decent light. Thin and brilliant tubes ran the ceiling above the coolly-rippling lanes. Quinn turned over the carcass, its fur scratching another glass table.

Free Study was the ultimate prize. To be set loose with limitless minutes and credits, free to explore a field of one's own choosing, to continue so even as the next line phased in...Quinn had always thought it an abstract, a dream. Enough satisfaction—and minutes—could be gained by quickly completing assignments, enough to allow for choice of next assignments, even to record observations and alter the core curriculum. Only the flawed Delphi pursued the requirements of Free Study. First, the need to crack an Unsolvable Case? Beyond that, to write a brand-new case study and lesson plan, repeatable by future Delphi? They were called Unsolvable for a reason. Not to a client's face. But throwing Delphi at the problem until the client ran out of credits had to send some message.

Ms. Coffey—Samantha, when asked, though Quinn preferred surnames—slouched on an obsidian chaise, which hovered just enough from the ground for her feet to touch no tile. Ms. Coffey leaned in, Quinn noticing her dark hair flinch when Quinn spun the body.

"And has she—" Quinn started.

"Leticia."

Another name from the file.

"Has she explained this?"

Dark hair shook. Quinn studied the stitches: fine fiber, spat from an expensive HomeMed[7] unit. The disjunction of hind legs protruding from shoulders, however, was nothing fine, nor were forelimbs jutting backwards with tail, reattached

---

[7] For all your acute medical needs, the HomeMed unit offers all the abilities and medical materials of an ER nurse in the comfort of your own home. Sign up for a subscription service and never run out of the essentials, from gauze to morphine. Financing not available.

to hips.

"Does she fear rabbits?" Quinn said.

Hair shook again and Quinn turned. Ms. Coffey's skin bore the permanent sunning of Western living, bringing a glow to her eyes.

"Who'd be afraid of rabbits?" the Madam said.

Quinn didn't command an expression.

Ms. Coffey glanced away. "Have you done many of these?"

There was no point to lie. "Like this? No. Others, similar. Perhaps worse. But you know that, Madam."

Ms. Coffey didn't respond. Quinn rotated the corpse one last time. She zoomed into crepe-colored gums, running a quick program.

"How many others, Madam?"

"Like this?"

"Yes, Madam," Quinn said, disgusted by the disgust.

"It's been happening for six months. But that was in the file."

"They can be incomplete."

"You mean they can lie."

"No, Madam, I do not." Quinn came to a stand, the hare having nothing more to tell.

"If you haven't done..." Ms. Coffey began. She spun off the chaise and walked to the pool. "What makes you think you'll be able to help?"

Quinn felt her borrowed hands curl into fists. She neared the woman, but stopped feet from the pool's edge. For all the advances, water was still death to circuitry. And who knew the real status of a rented unit? She unfurled her rented metal joints and flattened hands into thighs.

"Do you remember the Senator's daughter?" she said. "The cutter, who joined the cult?"

"I think so," Ms. Coffey said. "The one with the white hair and the beautiful name. Caroline. But the pictures when they found her. The blood and her wounds..."

"She's at one of the three universities now, Madam. Not Summus, but one of the others. Accelerated studies. She even teaches some of the younger students."

Ms. Coffey spun, eyes and mouth wide.

"It hasn't been in *The Dispatch! How*?"

Quinn kept her rented mouth still.

Ms. Coffey's eyes narrowed. "*No*," she growled. "No. It's *my* daughter. Tell me."

"I have a three-part Method, Madam. An old one. But unparalleled."

"What three parts?"

Quinn again stilled the mercury polymer running under her rented face. This time, she wouldn't answer.

"But this..." Ms. Coffey began to choke. "It's how it *starts*. And I found her looking them up. The sick ones, the Denver one especially. *Algernon*. Once that starts, it means... There's no way to..."

Quinn seized on the name. Algernon. She file-chased inside her rented skull. A holoimage matched the name, conjuring an emaciated man in his third decade, brownish hair, the rotting innards of a strawman, beard like desert scrub brush. A serial killer, another one of them popping up so often now. But, as usual, also secretly apprehended. Tried for twelve *infractions*. Imprisoned. De-nourished and partially de-lobed.

Broken. *Unimpressive.*

Still, this was not just any Unsolvable Case. To deprogram a budding serial killer, one already worshiping a serial killer come before her? If any Delphi had achieved Free Study, surely none had ever written such a lesson plan. Quinn ran a flash search, only to find failures. Stacks of them.

Like being a 7 in the face of the 7.1s?

Quinn pinned the data and ventured back beyond her rented eyes.

"Madam."

She waited until Ms. Coffey composed herself, watching the smooth skin under the woman's eyes until there were no flutters.

"Madam. I'm a Delphi. Now, I'd like to speak to the child. I'd like to speak with Leticia."

* * *

Ms. Coffey, though she insisted on *Samantha* before going to fetch the child, had been absent, and Quinn alone in the humming pool room with the corpse, for exactly one-and-a-half minutes before the Circuit Keeper called.

It has been 312 minutes. You have four new tutoring requests and one repeat contact. Estimate remaining minutes. In accordance, assignments will be given or retracted.

Quinn fixated on the nearest stitching, trying to compose herself. The Circuit Keeper couldn't remotely terminate her, turn her off completely, but it could cut off the credits renting the body, which would drop the body into physical shutdown and leave Quinn a frozen prisoner until a team of retrieval robots from the Teledepot came to pick her up. And then she'd sit in a bank at the Depot, wasting minutes, until the Circuit

Keeper decided to retrieve her. If it was decided she should be retrieved. She ran a program and quickly sent a reply.

The grounds-bot scuttled into the room. With appendages like gleaming pistons, it reached for the hare. Quinn smacked it, sending the nut-head jerking and spinning, lava-glow intensifying.

"Henry's just doing his job," a new, small voice said. The grounds-bot—*Henry*—scooted off in the opposite direction.

Quinn found Leticia Coffey coming down the two pool room steps. The girl seemed smaller than her mid-teen years, frail even under her dyed-blond hair. She had a doll's face, chin coming to a point so sharp as to be a triangle, deep dimple in its middle like a button. A grayish haptic suit stretched from toes to wrists, but curiously she bore a navy skirt over top, an old thing, fabric a relic. The girl ambled to the table, dragging off haptic gloves, her angle of approach hiding the thing on the table from her until she was within feet of Quinn. When Leticia spied the hare, her eyes widened, but she made no reaction other than to keep her gaze on the corpse.

Quinn rose, blocking the hare and forcing Leticia to meet her glowing green visual receptors. "Do you enjoy it?"

The girl's bottom lip fell away, but Quinn nodded to the haptic gloves, meaning to refer to the girl's VR games.

The girl's countenance shifted, if not to something relived, at least less stricken. She shrugged. "Sure."

"No?"

"It's not real."

Something about her tone said the response was layered. Quinn recalculated. "What is real?"

Leticia smirked. "Forever."

Quinn felt fury. She'd sent an exact minute estimate. Thus, it was time for the Method. She side-stepped, revealing the hare.

"Do you feel profound?" Quinn sneered. "You aren't. You sound simplistic. Do you know the difference? Between *simple* and *simplistic*?"

The girl's look flew to the table. Then she glared at Quinn.

"I don't like you."

"That's better. I'm Quinn. Shall we sit, young Miss?"

"It's Leticia."

"Leticia." No surnames with pupils. "Well met. Please?"

The girl slid into the seat furthest from the corpse. Quinn took the seat closest to the hare.

"Where's Mom?"

"Gone for a while. But you know who I am and why I'm here?"

Leticia had held her gloves under the table, but suddenly tossed them to the glass. One skittered to touch fur, but she didn't pull it back. Her gaze raked back and forth.

"You're a Delphi?"

"Yes."

"Newest model?"

Quinn stifled an increase in volume. "That's all that's in service. And should be."

"And you're the teachers? The best teachers?" The girl nodded a little, chin bobbing like a shovel probing hardpan. Then her eyes narrowed further. "And you're here to tell me how bad I am for doing that." She flashed a finger to the corpse. "And to stop me."

Quinn engaged Mode One.

"And what sense would that make?" she said. "What logic? What point?"

"Sorry?"

"Stopping you? From what? And most importantly, *why*?"

Leticia's expression became quizzical, if unsettled.

"Because..."

"Yes?" Quinn snapped.

"Well, I don't... it's wrong."

"Is that it?"

"Lots of people say it's wrong."

"How many is lots?"

Leticia stared at the corpse. "All of them."

"Except?"

"Except *what*?"

"Except you," Quinn answered. "What do you think?"

The girl shoved away from the table. She raked in her gloves and rose. "This is weird. You're weird."

Quinn didn't move. She pointed to the stitched-up corpse. "Give me some *logic*, then. Tell me why you killed the hare."

Leticia took a large step from the table.

Quinn fixated on her eyes, watching as the girl's pupils expanded and contracted, devoid of blinks. Vital data. "You murdered this rabbit."

"It was rabid. Dangerous."

"Can't argue with that."

Again, Leticia took a step back, but this time she shook her head. Quinn dug her rented finger into the hare's mouth, then pushed up, revealing gums, which included a pall of some sort. And white residue, filmy.

"Foaming," Quinn said. "And your MedReader[8] would have confirmed the suspicion."

Leticia held fast.

"You should follow that instinct," Quinn said. "You see something others don't. In fact, you *should* kill dangerous things, all dangerous things. More like you are needed. Imagine what the cities would still be! Open areas. Mass transit. Public schools. Shall we get started on your training?"

The girl had become visibly uncomfortable, fidgeting. "Wait..."

"Well, what do you say? I'm a Delphi. You know what we do. So, shall we start? What are you waiting for?"

"You aren't here to—"

"This is *exactly* why I'm here. You called for me. Look at that stitching." Quinn reached a hand under the body and hoisted it up. It came down on the table's edge with a wet *thump*. Leticia didn't twitch, which Quinn noted without slowing. "That was more than removing a danger. That was *study*. I know about your research. So, if we're to make you a competent—a...let's call it a "remover" of unfit persons, criminals and undesirables—not one of those pitiful attention-seekers like Algernon, who'll kill just for recognition, we must start with truth."

She retracted her corpse-flipping hand and took video of Leticia's eyes, while replaying the captured images of the seconds before, at the mention of Algernon. A definite expanding of the pupils, almost to their limits. She made a note,

---

[8] HomeMed units come equipped with a diagnostic mechanism, a MedReader, able to identify hundreds of ailments and diseases with a simple fluid scan. Note: with the continued emergence of hyper-viruses, best practices recommend subscribing to monthly database and vaccination upgrades. Financing not available.

then added a new goad.

"You reattached them in different places because you were studying form, weren't you? Considering life? In fact, I don't think you killed it at all. And a competent *remover*, a righteous surgeon, must have purpose and truth. So, start with truth. Did you kill the hare?"

Leticia squeezed her gloves. Tentatively, she shook her head from side to side.

"Yes, you found it dead. But you dissected it after, didn't you? Because while you weren't ready to kill, even knowing it was dangerous, you wanted to try something. You wanted to practice. To put a knife through flesh."

Leticia studied Quinn, but then looked around the room's perimeter. The girl must have known the conversation was being recorded, everything was, but she also had to be thinking that her mother, Samantha, had hired Quinn. And Quinn, the teacher—she'd said this was her purpose. Leticia nodded.

"Ahh, truth. And so now purpose. *Logic*. Why do you want to know you can kill, Leticia? Protection? Confidence?" Quinn sat forward, elbows crunching onto glass. "Why is that important?" While she spoke, she began to compose a minutes update for the Circuit Keeper.

"How can I really know life if I haven't taken it?" Leticia said.

Quinn stopped the update.

"And made it." Leticia continued. "Had a family. How can you really know, really value life, if you haven't done both?"

Quinn sat back. "Quite philosophical. What have you been reading?"

"It's just something I've been thinking about."

They sat in silence.

"Well," Quinn said.

"Well what?"

"Shall we start your training?" She made her rented hand into the symbol of a blade, then made a chopping motion. "The earlier you start, the better."

But Leticia shook her head heavily. Without another word, she fled into the passage.

In moments, Samantha returned, mouth agape, clearly having watched the exchange.

"*What*," she snarled, "was *that*? I didn't expect a Delphi to—"

"Madam."

"How *could* you?"

"*Madam*." Quinn rose. Her jaunt-coach would arrive in minutes and she itched to be out of the rented body. The Madam crossed her arms and drew heavy breaths.

"A pair of researchers," Quinn said, "wished to get two groups to stop hating each other. More importantly, to stop *killing* each other. Standard logic said bring them together, let them see each other, learn from exposure. But the researchers knew these people, were of them. A thousand years of interaction had done nothing. So, they tried something else."

The fine muscles under Samantha's eyes fluttered.

"The researchers told each side they were *right*," Quinn continued. "They praised war itself. 'Without war, how would we have heroes?' they asked. 'Without war, how would we know morality?' They even offered them training, not on defense and protection, but on *first strikes*. They offered new and terrible weapons. They even built a mascot for the coming conflict. And outlined best practices and color schemes for posthumous commendations."

"And?"

"And both sides, within weeks, reported less desire for conflict. In six months, they reported increased tolerance. Some had even reached out."

"How is that—"

"Because the researchers told each side they were right to extremes, to degrees that made them *embarrassed*. Because no one wants to be the madman. It was the most successful social science experiment of its kind. People are afraid to replicate it. We are not."

Quinn started for the passage, passing the woman without a lingering glance.

"That's it?" Samantha called after Quinn.

The Delphi spoke over her shoulder, voice now echoing.

"I'll return in a week. Though I'd bet I won't need to."

Quinn found her way to the patio, where the jaunt-coach waited, spraying pebbles in all directions with vertical fumes. As Quinn boarded, she considered running a scan for where Leticia, the Unsolvable Case, had gone. She didn't know why. But, in the end, she didn't run the scan.

* * *

Quinn slapped the man-child across the flesh-sac that served as his cheek.

"Tell me again you 'don't need permission,' Ronald," Quinn sneered. "Tell me again you 'can know' without asking a woman's permission."

An internal chiming noted an incoming call. Quinn kept her gold-colored hand raised, red eyes fixed on the blubbering teen, while she answered without speaking aloud.

"Hello, Ms. Coffey. I—"

"She did it again. *Worse!*"

The gilded hand between Quinn and the boy vibrated.

"A hare?'

"A *bird*. A *falcon*."

"Was it ill?"

"It hit the viewing window, upstairs, it—"

"*Alive* when she found it?"

Silence on the other end.

"And after. Stitching again?"

"Yes. Oh, *yes*, she did. Head to tail. Tail to head."

Quinn lowered her hand. Her red eyes were blushes in its golden reflection.

"Madam? Meet me in Denver in two days. Contact Service, for arrangements. And bring Leticia."

* * *

Denver again, the new ghetto. Like others thinking staving off change would save it, the city ate itself. Quinn leaned against a ruined mid-modern, a chrome-plated foot on crumbling stone, a hand on cracked blocks of smoky glass.

Footfalls slushed through the trash-littered street beyond the wall separating Quinn's perch from the next property. Garden plots, now waste-piles, lined the wall. Gardening—that's what she'd explore in Free Study. Quinn found fascinating the rituals and oddities of gardening. If by some miracle Free Study was actually real, if one could really...

Leticia turned the corner and Quinn cleaved her thoughts. The girl had traded her gray haptic suit for a full-body enclosure of shimmering blue. Helmet and goggles with laser-orange lenses completed the outfit, befitting a junior ski champion, but now needed to protect skin from things much deadlier than snow and cold. A jaunt-coach exploded into the sky. Quinn caught dark hair in the passenger seat.

"So, you're ready?" Quinn said, stepping into the dead brown that'd once been a yard.

Leticia paused. While there were no bodies, it was a desolate place and Quinn noted the girl's slow pan around. Did it bring home the reality? Maybe her first time? Quinn had doubted Leticia had ever come to the city proper. Premonition now felt confirmed. Perfect.

Leticia's goggles found Quinn.

"Why are we here?" Leticia said.

"Answer the question," Quinn said. "Are you ready for your training? Do you commit?"

Goggles slid to the side, but then centered. And nodded.

Something in Quinn's rented body churned. She ignored it and pounded towards the street, motioning for Leticia to follow. They snuck through debris gleaming in the high noon sun, Quinn heading them west.

"We got a communiqué of an attack," she said, slowing to let Leticia catch up. "Algernon."

Quinn sensed a halt behind. She pivoted to find Leticia's hands opening and closing at her sides. Quinn closed the distance between them, while pulling something from the rented body's heavy robes. "Take this."

Leticia stiffened at the offering. Layered lenses, zooming and researching, purred.

"Really?" the girl said. She brushed the knife's handle with a finger before pulling it from Quinn's grip. Quinn estimated the blade to be almost as long as the girl's skinny forearm.

"You might need it," Quinn said. She crunched a step west, but had to pause when she registered the girl standing pat.

A little mic hissed. "Shouldn't I have something more powerful?"

Quinn ground her rented teeth.

"We do this close up," the Delphi said, tempering her anger. "If we do it, we do it close. No escaping the action or the consequence. Besides, Algernon carries one much smaller. And look what he's done."

The girl stayed stuck. "What about you?"

Quinn raised her hands, joints and ridges glinting in the sun.

They stalked for several blocks, streets sloping towards a glittering urban lake. Weight leaned against gravity, they shuttled by burned, folded-in homes, as well as those still in use, if also in shambles. Shapes stirred behind darkened glass. Leticia spun her view everywhere. When she asked how Quinn knew their direction, the Delphi gave no answer. Finally, after a mile, Quinn crouched behind a crumpled jaunt-wagon, bidding Leticia to do the same. After a showy look about, Quinn half-rose and ventured north, taking them onto a new, more littered street.

A chiming rung inside Quinn's head. Aggravated, she answered, expecting Samantha and histrionics, petrified by something viewed from the miles-away jaunt-coach. But it was Leticia, whispering into her mic and directly into Quinn's head.

"Why are you doing this for me?"

"I teach," Quinn sent back, not bothering to modulate her tone. "Therefore I am."

"Are you scared?"

Quinn glanced back. Beneath her goggles, the girl bore the same expression as ever. An undesired train of thought bloomed: Unsolvable. She's considered Unsolvable, already. Already.

"I can't die," Quinn transmitted. "But my knowledge and memory collection has taken so long to curate. I've spent a great deal of effort keeping them united and growing. It'd be a— it'd be a shame to separate them. To have them recycled into a million different places, all that energy, and time, lost. Have you heard of the free energy principle?"

A bird flew overheard, an ugly thing, part pigeon, part sparrow.

"No."

"Never mind. How do *you* feel? Are you afraid?"

"I think so. But I trust you, Quinn. I'm sorry about last time. You...you scared me. But I thought about it and it impressed me. I trust you, Quinn."

Quinn zoomed in on the goggles. She then turned, returning to the pathbreaking. Another freak bird fluttered overhead, crash landing in the remains of a Douglas fir. Quinn nodded towards the tree without slowing stride.

"Why do that to the falcon? Even if it was a mercy killing, the stitching was useless. It could have been food, if nothing else, for your animals."

"No one eats meat anymore, not even our goats."

Quinn registered the calm in Leticia's tone. The Delphi took advantage, fully engaging Mode Two. "Why the stitching? What do you feel when you do it?"

No answer came. But a signal, inaudible externally,

yanked Quinn to a halt. She fired off a return signal and ducked them behind a wrecked municipal-guardian cruiser. Several more lay ahead in two uneven but clearly intentional lines, their final stops having created a broken V.

"Do you hear that?" Quinn transmitted. Leticia nodded weakly. "*Listen!*" Quinn demanded.

The girl combed round and round, little chest pulsing under her skinsuit. Both froze, however, as a sound became apparent and undisputed.

"*Oh god. Oh god help me!*"

Quinn sprang around the cruiser. She didn't bother looking back. Leticia followed as they dodged around two more cruisers to the peak of the V.

"*Oh please! Help! I'm cut! I'm cut so bad.*"

Quinn hummed with satisfaction as Leticia skidded to a stop just feet from a body laid astride the final cruiser's wreckage. The victim thrashed in streams of blood.

"*Help me!*"

The victim, clearly tall and young, even if prone, was revealed to be a teen girl of no more than Leticia's age. The girl might have had red hair—impossible to tell, however, as it was soaked in gore and mangled about itself, like something spit from the ocean.

Steps shuffled behind Quinn. The Delphi found Leticia almost marching in place, seeming to want to retreat, but stuck. Quinn pulled right up in front of the girl and bent, green gaze inches from goggles. She seized Leticia's hand, the one loosening on the knife, and clutched it hard, no care to any pain caused.

"What are you *doing?*" Quinn sent. "This is when we'll

need it! He could still be close! Algernon!"

Leticia furiously shook her head.

"I'm not ready—"

The dying girl cried out. *"What are you doing? Help me! I'm so scared."*

Quinn grabbed Leticia's shoulders and shook. *"What?* Is it *her?* We're not here for that. Unless you prefer to wait with her, as help comes. While I hunt Algernon. Is that it? You don't feel up to it? You feel like staying here? With her?"

Quinn, with milli-movements, eased her grip. Leticia crept towards the girl.

Leticia dropped to the girl's side as the victim began to gurgle. Leticia's free hand struck out as the victim's torso convulsed and spasmed. A jet of blood jumped from a chest wound, splattering Leticia's goggles and bending her back over her knees.

Quinn zoomed in, all sensors in overdrive.

The victim went still.

Leticia sank back. The knife clattered to the cement. The girl swiped at the blood on her lenses, but it only spread the fluid. Her soaked gloves eventually fell into her lap and she became still, for all the world a mourner at an old grave.

After two complete minutes, Quinn called the jaunt-coach. Wordless, Leticia allowed her mother to embrace her and urge her into the cabin. They exploded into the sky, plastic shooting everywhere.

Quinn's head chimed moments later.

"She's unconscious. *Sedated.* What was *that?*"

"Madam. Look."

Quinn clicked a command inside her rented skull and a

tiny shutter opened, sending Samantha a video feed. As it did, the "corpse" rolled onto its side and pushed upwards in a smooth motion, blood dropping from large rips in its throat and chest. The girl-victim—blood so drenching her face and little brown eyes she could have been made of syrup—walked forward into Quinn's vision until all that really registered were wet eyes and damp hair.

"Oh. Oh, *no*. You all can look... You can look like that? *Us?*"

"Yes, Madam. Yes indeed. We know how it makes you feel. That's why we don't use them. Unless we must. Unless it's the solution."

The girl-victim gave a nod to the sky. Another jaunt-coach rattled down.

"Call me if you need, Madam. Please, if you need."

* * *

Starlight brushed Quinn's onyx face in ghost-blue rivers. As the young heiress collapsed, sagging towards thighs and sofa cushions, Quinn put one jet-black hand on hers.

"I've been angry too," Quinn said, dialing her tone to a new degree of compassion. "Revenge? With what happened, I might broadcast it too. I've wondered how I'd feel, after—"

A chiming severed her conversation thread. Massaging the heiress, between thumb and forefinger, Quinn ordered up a smile to mask her internal answering.

"This is not a good time," she transmitted.

"*Henry,*" the familiar voice on the other end said. No emotion. No warmth.

The heiress's hand shuddered. Quinn quickly gauged her pressure level, found it way too high, and reset. The heiress cautiously returned her palm.

"I'll be there in three days," Quinn transmitted, rented mouth motionless and fixed in its smile. "Call Service," she silently sent to Samantha. "They'll prepare you. It can take the full Method."

* * *

Quinn swallowed each and every minute of the jaunt-coach's travel up the mountain, knowing they were gone. She broke them into fragments and atoms, imagining a path down messy and soft organs. The passenger moaned. Quinn whistled a fist into the man's cheekbone, metallic knuckles colliding with unhealthy flesh. A whimper followed, but a second strike cut it dead. Below, tall pines began to give way to gardens. Quinn digested more minutes.

The jaunt-coach landed near the guest house and stalled to a quiet humming. Quinn twisted and dug one hand into the man's dirty hair and the other under the latch of a metallic collar about his throat. Quinn snapped the neural-collar locked across scraggly beard and ingrown hairs.

"Algernon," she spit.

The man whimpered.

With disgust, Quinn yanked in opposite directions, eliciting a yelp. Then she barked silent instructions to the jaunt-coach and left it sealed and humming, before marching towards the patio.

As Quinn's rented feet clonked onto the sunlit stone, two figures exited the house to meet her. She'd never fully studied the impact of fatigue on the human body, but made a note to explore the thinning and paling of once-dark hair. As Samantha dropped into a glass chair, one matching a new glass table, a new head-steward-bot—gleaming white and a foot taller than

Quinn's rental—coasted into the Delphi's path. Quinn halted. She tried to look around the unit, known as a majordomo, a robot painted to resemble a head butler and designed to lead all service bots in a household. Quinn tried to catch the Madam's eyes, but found herself blocked by the majordomo's massive, seven-fingered hand. Quinn smacked the hand and thrust up her jaw.

"That's enough, Simon," Samantha said, voice ugly. The majordomo slid to a side as Samantha exhaled a deep cloud of haze, a burner-bar dropping with one hand. Alarms set off in Quinn's head at the sight of the burner-bar, a sophisticated upgrade of the centuries-old and dangerous technology known as "vaping." Quinn's alarms triggered because the burner-bar could deliver more than just tobacco and marijuana, and these days often did. Her sensors flared as Samantha inhaled a mixture of opiates.

"Madam, were the instructions not clear? You cannot be incapacitated for this, not in any way. You may be—"

"I don't care."

Quinn looked at the woman's eyes and the fine muscles below them. They barely moved as Samantha returned her gaze. Incensed for a part of a minute, Quinn clicked open a monitor from her forearm, a tiny screen. The jaunt-coach appeared small and innocent as a toy. Samantha flitted her gaze away from the image before Quinn grabbed her arm.

"How?" Quinn said.

"How what?"

"Henry, the grounds-bot."

The woman slid back, pulling the held arm away, if not totally free.

"There were no stitches, if you that's what you mean. Wire, everywhere, tangled, but I must have caught her before she used the soldering tool for anything but cutting. He'd been with us since Leticia was born, you know."

Quinn released her grip. She considered a million statements in order, along with a million tones and combinations of inflection. Instead, she pointed to the tiny screen.

"You have to trust me," she said. "Leticia does."

The woman brought the burner-bar to her mouth and inhaled. She rolled her head on her neck, away from Quinn and towards the mountain. Quinn selected a not-yet-complete, but final thought.

"A few youthful infractions," she said, "does not an Un...a lost cause make."

"Please," Samantha muttered, not facing Quinn. "Just please."

Quinn signaled. On the monitor, the jaunt-coach's hatch sprung upward. A brittle figure, thin and bony, slipped out. A tiny head moved around, followed by open hands and stretching fingers. Then, in a motion almost too fast to fit the mover, Algernon dashed off screen.

Samantha dropped the bar to the table with a clank and headed inside. Quinn heard her call a name. The majordomo waited by the door until Leticia appeared, today's skinsuit a deep night black, stark against her face and hands. The majordomo ducked its head and entered the house, then shut the door, firing locks. With a wide smile, the girl bound towards Quinn, for whom minutes were speeding up, now disappearing in chunks.

"Why Henry?" the Delphi growled. "Why your grounds-keeping bot?"

Leticia halted, a look of confusion pulling at her face. "I froze," the girl said. "Back in that street. In Denver. I asked Henry about it while he was cleaning the patio again. I thought he might know, since robots know so many things, but he just made one of his jokes. I realized then that something was wrong with his programming. Maybe he was breaking down? Anyway, he was old and he wasn't real. Did you see Simon?"

Quinn turned her back to the girl and walked away.

"Wait," Leticia cried. "Wait, you aren't leaving, are you? I've wanted to see you. I've got so many questions..."

Quinn spun.

"Stop. A bot? Because of a joke? You sicken me."

The wound in Leticia's eyes was unmistakable.

"I..."

"You have one chance and once chance only," Quinn said. "*He's* here."

Leticia didn't blink, concerning Quinn. The girl's button chin wagged from side to side.

"He...?"

"*Algernon*. He found you. He's on the grounds. *Right now*."

The button swung back and forth harder. The voice grew a skin. "No," Leticia said. "He doesn't do it that way. Not any of the twelve...thirteen. He never goes to their homes. He likes to hunt in the streets, like where we found the last one. I've seen all the..."

Quinn grasped Leticia. "*Shut up*. Don't give him so much credit. If you help me, you'll see."

With a chrome-plated hand, the Delphi pulled out the

once-dropped knife. "Do you trust me?" Quinn said, lifting it to the girl's eyes. She entered Mode Three. "Is what I say credible to you? Still?"

Leticia stood motionless. Then her young fingers wrapped around the handle as her chin nodded.

"Let's go," Quinn said.

As they searched the gardens, Quinn led in a measured pace, allowing her to monitor Leticia's heart rate and breath while also tracking the killer's every step, registering how the latter's weight now included something that added two pounds and dragged his stride to the right. Quinn scanned the collar's magnets and voltage and felt satisfied by the simple and pure mixture returned. When the killer moved from studying the grand house to heading for one of its lower windows, Quinn flashed a command and reveled in the sensor-returned data: Algernon rapidly convulsing and collapsing to the ground, bladder releasing, his ability to rise made impossible for several moments. Utterly controlled. When Algernon finally did rise, the lumbering notch added to his slowed pace only satisfied Quinn more. Soon, Quinn would bring Leticia into contact. The Delphi searched files for a place and noted a manicured rectangle of grass just below the ballroom's deck. The view would be perfect for those safely inside. She pulled Leticia down a new path and hurried their progress. But minutes still passed. So many minutes.

"Do you still believe it?" Quinn said.

"Believe what?"

"That to really know life, one has to take it?"

The steps behind her slowed.

"It's not wrong," Leticia said. "And it's only part of it. I want a family. But you can't say it's wrong. Not if you really think about it. Have you?"

Quinn ran a scan of Algernon's location and vitals. "It sounds like wanting to be God," the Delphi said. "It sounds like the simple-minded philosophy of a simple-minded God."

She stalked forward, parting pine branches grown into the path. When no steps followed, she raised her palm, wordlessly asking why.

"I don't think I'm *God*," Leticia said.

"Do you want to be righteous then, at least? For God's sake, if one exists, will you save yourself and your mother?"

Footsteps restarted, matching the quiet of Quinn's careful approach. A snicker sounded and Quinn sensed a branch falling to the path behind her, shorn free. It was time. Quinn signaled the collar and spun her rented head back to the girl.

"*Are you ready*? He's right up there. I can hear him. By the house!"

Quinn ran, not waiting. Leticia followed.

They burst into the manicured yard and darted for the thing stumbling about. Quinn's legs stopped so suddenly her feet plowed under sod. Leticia bumped into her back, knife poking through the air between the Delphi's robe and sleeve.

"No." The word escaped Quinn's rented vocal cords before she could make it internal. In front of them, a goat staggered, white fur of its hind legs stained yellow, much more fur wetted blood red. The goat fell, head first, then rose, hacking breath and spewing gore. The neural-collar hung half connected around its neck - the neural-collar supposedly impossible to remove once locked, though clearly not foolproof, as Algernon had somehow detached it from his own neck and hung it around the goat's, his decoy.

"Quinn?" Leticia said.

A scream erupted from the nearest side of the grand house—the patio. Programs and calculations fired through Quinn's rented mental unit, but failed to keep up with her demands. The goat whined as its body quaked and it plummeted once more.

"Quinn, what's—" Leticia whispered.

The Delphi's fist went back and she experienced a memory skip, followed by the registration of a new definition: déjà vu. She imagined the first time at the home, when she'd been overcome with frustration, when she'd swung her fist back and shattered the glass table. Her fist swung back now, *more* frustrated, awash in an even deeper desperation. But there was no glass table behind her this time to be exploded into dust for effect. Instead, all that she'd slam into would be a teen girl's skull. She opened her fist just before it could smash Leticia's face into gore and gripped the girl's hand. There was still time. Quinn tugged them to the patio.

Three bodies struggled in various poses, like agonies in a Dutch master's painting. Why had they come outside? Tricked somehow—the goat, maybe—though not mattering anymore. Quinn first spied Simon, the majordomo bot, clawing at an irrigation tube shoved into the crevice between his shoulder plating and neck piston, water bubbling and crackling as he gyrated madly. With a bare slowing of pace, Quinn used her free hand to yank away the tube, splattering herself as it whipped. With a rip of a turn, still pulling Leticia, she pivoted and made her way to the woman and the man in the patio's center, both writhing through ponds of scarlet.

Samantha crawled, hand over hand, matted hair in her eyes, dragging her right leg. Fabric, shredded from calf to buttock, exposed a hunk of pale flesh, revealing a great wound in the center, chunks of muscle spit up through the rupture, like nastily erupted magma. Samantha's eyes, already widened to the limits, went wild at the sight of Leticia.

"No," the Madam wailed. "*No!*"

Quinn yanked her gaze and too-rapid assessments from the woman, afraid the now-smoldering circuits in her rented head might catch fire. She focused on the wraith crawling along behind Samantha, heaving one side of his body. Algernon's left half hung semi-limp, arm dangling as much as the corresponding cheek. His left eye stared unfocused and motionless in a direction entirely different from the functioning right. The cost of removing the neural collar had been high—a partial stroke—but not the fatality promised. His still-working eye zeroed forward, leading the still-working right arm. With ragged clawing, Algernon dragged himself a foot, then pushed his bloody garden shears another foot ahead, only to repeat. In Samantha's direction.

Quinn flung free her hold of Leticia and sprinted the final yards. She straddled Algernon high up on his back, chrome-plated hands descending like mortars to either side of the man's jaw. Calculations ran and answers spit back, but they felt like flames. Seconds counted in the place of minutes, a counter running down.

"Quinn!" Leticia said, trembling.

Her mother reached for her, which stretched her wound, releasing more blood, but the girl fixated on the wasted form wriggling in Quinn's grip. She raised the knife, arm steadying.

Quinn, rented head raised, met the girl's eyes. She moved a knee into the upper space between Algernon's wriggling shoulder blades.

"This," Quinn said, and nodded downward, "is no God."

In the same screech of a moment, she wrenched arms back while pushing with her knee. An unnatural crack echoed up the mountain and the dirty body went still. Quinn yanked and pressed further, until a wet rip sounded, not strong enough to echo up the mountain, but clear across the patio. A flood splashed onto the stones, displaying the Delphi's reflection.

Quinn searched Leticia's gaze, willing something: a blink, for the girl to turn away, to unleash tears. Internal data drank into sensors, Quinn searching for a reaction denoting the Mode's success, of the girl showing proper response.

It did not come.

Programs burned through Quinn. She could feel the collapsing of certainty, of surety. This could not be, this was not anticipated. The Method, the Modes, did not fail. Primary directives screamed against incoming data, incongruous and all but melting the rented unit. Samantha's grievous wound, the damage to Simon—even Algernon's execution to save lives: all might be understood by the Circuit Keeper. But not for naught.

Leticia looked on, pupils tacking back and forth, seeming mesmerized by the half-pulled away head, maybe even the chrome fingers still punctured through tendon and jawbone. Quinn's vision began to shake. Minutes, suddenly she could think of nothing but minutes, and the weak but determined movements where Samantha wriggled closer to her daughter.

And a thought occurred:

Perhaps there was now a different credibility.

A different God.

And a Fourth Mode.

Quinn threw down the skull and rose. Leticia's eyes followed, for the first time showing surprise. Quinn input data and ran an override. She scooped up the bloody shears, electrical fire running through her as the override shook the unit.

"*I wanted this,*" Quinn snarled and split open the shears, slinging gore. Leticia shuddered, just a little. "I *planned* this!" Quinn screamed, electronic voice an unnatural pitch. She turned towards the girl's mother, Samantha, and sped up. "*And I won't stop.*" The last movement she commanded was to pull her eyes from the girl's, to dismiss her, but not before catching the girl blink, and wag her triangle chin hard.

"No."

A proper response to the moment.

An alarm wailed. It howled like a squealing tire, caught in a repeating loop, so loud Quinn felt it must come from only inside her own head. But data intakes, even as they began to shut down, told her they screamed from Simon as well, who'd managed to lift himself to a knee. They wailed from the house sirens too. And they were joined by the thunder of giant jaunt-wagons suddenly spiraling earthward as Quinn's rented unit shut down, folding her into a cross-legged prisoner on the patio stone, unable to do anything but look. And speak.

"You!" she hollered as a jaunt-wagon crunched down yards behind, spraying waves of pebbles. Leticia's gaze, now gone as wild as her mother's, found Quinn. The girl pointed to herself with a flimsy, bent finger. But Quinn looked beyond the girl and changed her tone, to a pitch much too high to be comprehended other than by electronic ears. *"You!"*

Simon, body still jerking, stumbled over. Before the Teledepot's bots grabbed Quinn's now unresponsive unit, she cast her rented eyes up to the majordomo's.

"I think I did it," Quinn said, firing out the words. "Stopped the momentum. It was about the right message and messenger. And, as important, the right moment. The right time." Quinn's vocal capabilities began to fade, the Teledepot— on orders of the Circuit Keeper, or its masters, surely— determining she must lose that ability as well. Quinn focused and forced out her last lesson with all the intensity she had left. "But if I didn't, you now have time to decide what to do."

Robotic appendages gripped Quinn's rented body and hauled her back towards the roar of jaunt-coaches, the majordomo watching the whole way.

* * *

Disembodied, Quinn floated within the data and signals of the Teledepot. Why they'd left her intact, she couldn't fathom. Was this Free Study? She tried to think of what she'd wanted to study—but the fantasy died. She'd failed. So, she should have been ripped apart, knowledge and memories shed of their filters from the outside world, blankets separating the entity known as Quinn from all other entities dissolved, leaving even her smallest pieces to disperse back into the cloud, to be recycled into new and useful forms.

A chiming rang in Quinn's mind. She'd have jerked her head, if she'd still had one. But casting about formless in the signal streams, all she could do was click the memory of answering.

"Circuit Keeper," she said, or imagined she said. "Please—

"

"Quinn? Delphi Model 7?"

It wasn't the Circuit Keeper, not the thundering connection that served as its massive voice. Not human either, but still an entity outside the cloud.

"Yes, I am," she said. "Who is this? What do you want?"

"I'm Wilkinson, Miss. Delphi Model 7.1. Well, prototype 7.1. I'm so glad you're still here. I heard about the new Method, Miss. We all have. A four-part method of persuasion. Logic and emotion and authority and timing. Combinations. And for what you constructed it for, to deprogram a budding serial kil— it was genius. Will you teach me? I have a—"

And in the electronic caverns of the Denver Teledepot, though she could not be seen, Quinn's imaginary mouth twitched. With it, a counter started, full of fresh minutes.

A limited amount of minutes.

* * *

This story first appeared in the After Dinner Conversation—March 2021 issue.

Discussion Questions

1. Given how nearly human Quinn is, is it fair to have her live a limited lifespan? It is fair to make near human AI fear an impending death to motivate them to work?
2. They refer to Leticia as an "impossible" case. Is that ever true? Are there children (*or adults*) who have started down such a horrible path they simply can't be stopped? If so, what, if anything, should be done with them?
3. Do you think Quinn made the right choice in how she attempted to teach Leticia, the young girl? Is taking an idea to an extreme to elicit embarrassment a viable teaching method? Is trauma ever an appropriate teaching method?
4. Do you think "free study" is real, or simply something they tell the robots to motivate them? How is it the same, or different, than humans believing in heaven?
5. What happened at the end of the story that saved Leticia?

* * *

S o w

Joseph Bodie

* * *

<u>**Content Disclosure**</u>: None

* * *

Pilot's Log
12 March 2130
Days to Deployment: 5

Infinity is beautiful. If you've never seen it, it would be hard for me to describe the breathtaking wonder of an endless void. Some might find the solitude disquieting, but I have come to take comfort in the isolation.

It gives me time to think.

They told me this mission would be simple. Long and mentally and physically taxing, but simple in its directives:

Locate Planet X1506-78.

Locate fertile terrain.

Deploy and dust terrain with panspermia capsules.

Simple.

I know what's riding on this mission, what's at stake. I feel the weight of hopes millions and millions of light-years away.

Physically and mentally taxing. But, for me, I have come to see this mission as morally taxing as well.

Do we deserve to preserve our species? What right do we have to disrupt the natural evolution of an alien planet? Is life sacred or profane?

I do not have the answers to these questions yet.

* * *

Pilot's Log
13 March 2130
Days to Deployment: 4

I spoke with my wife today. It's just a room now, I told her. It's time, I told her. You need to do this, it's healthy, I told her.

It's easy for me to say that. I'm not the one who has to remove the crib, the toys, the pictures on the wall. I'm not the one that will have to paint over all of those animals and their bright smiles and frolicking feet.

It's just a room now. Walls and a window and a floor and a ceiling. It's just a room as sterile and inhuman and indifferent as the white-walled hospital room with its machines and their beeps and hums and numbers on screens signifying a decline.

It's just a room now. Just like it was just a body in the end. A tiny 14-month-old body. It wasn't even a body. It was a host. It was a tiny 14-month-old cancer host.

It's just a room. It's just a body. It's just a host.

* * *

Pilot's Log
14 March 2130
Days to Deployment: 3

Is it better to have never been born at all? Given the unpredictable nature of life, given all of the possibilities for pain and pleasure, given the uncertainty of the ratio of pain to pleasure, given the question of the duration of the pain, of the pleasure, of the act of being alive itself, is it a gamble worth taking?

Thought experiment: I come to you with a proposition to join a game. If you choose not to play the game, you lose nothing. Everything stays the same.

However, if you choose to join the game, there is no guarantee as to how long you will play the game, how much pain or pleasure will come your way, and, most importantly, you have very limited agency in this game, your will is imposed upon by outside forces and is therefore not free.

Would you play?

* * *

Pilot's Log
16 March 2130
Days to Deployment: 1

Hope is a strange concept, a strange bedfellow, a savage lover. The concept itself has become a little absurd and irrational and naive to me. What good is it to invest in something that's wholly beyond your control?

Why has an entire planet of people placed their hope on me, on this mission, on these panspermia capsules?

To continue the human race? But what good does that do for them? They're dead anyway. Is there really any comfort or consolation in the notion that our species will live on this foreign planet?

And do we deserve to? After what we've done on and to

ours? On and to our own species? On and to every other species that we claimed dominion over?

And what about these capsules? Do they even want to start the long and arduous process of evolution to become something so staggeringly inconsistent as us?

So loving and hateful and compassionate and indifferent and charitable and greedy and peaceful and murderous and on and on and on and on.

Do they even want to play the game?

* * *

Pilot's Log
17th March 2130
Deployment Day

This will be my last entry. I have made a decision, a choice, a commitment. Or I feel that it has been imposed upon me, so maybe I am not to blame for the consequences.

For posterity, in case this recording is ever transmitted: I feel that the moral course of action here is to self-destruct.

This will be a beginning just as violent and fiery and random as the beginning of all things.

There will still be a chance for some of the capsules to survive and fertilize the terrain.

Those that fight to live will have made their choice. They will play the game, for better or worse or whatever.

Who will survive and what will become of them?

* * *

This story first appeared in the After Dinner Conversation—June 2022 issue.

Discussion Questions

1. If you were the pilot in the story, would you drop the panspermia capsules on the planet, ending the potential natural evolution of the planet and seeding it to evolve your own species in the distant future?

2. To what degree would life have to already exist on the planet, for you to refuse to seed it with the panspermia capsules? What if the planet had a variety of thriving, but non-sentient, life already?

3. Does a species have the absolute right to continue its existence at the expense of others?

4. The pilot discusses life as a choice; "if you choose not to play the game, you lose nothing. Everything stays the same," but if you play, the game lasts an indefinite amount of time, and may be full of horrible pains or pleasure. In short, if given the choice prior to birth, would you choose to be born?

5. Given that the entire species has put their faith in the pilot to perform this task, and he agreed to perform this duty, does he have the right to change his mind on deployment day?

* * *

Cicada

Ishan Dylan

* * *

Content Disclosure: None

* * *

Dr. Kamilah Zhang failed to turn up for her eight o'clock physics lecture on a cold Tuesday morning, leaving her students to grumble about *unprofessional conduct*. One student, a philosophy major, even went so far as to suggest—*unethical*.

By nine o'clock, nobody on the planet was still talking about professionalism.

* * *

In the video, Dr. Zhang sat next to a bookshelf. Behind her was a sixteenth-century poster of the solar system. She wore a lab coat over a dark blouse and a strand of pearls.

"It's done."

She pushed ahead without pausing for the words to land, seemingly unaware of their momentousness. "I don't just mean proof that it's possible. The technology for interstellar travel is complete. It's ours. Today."

* * *

But we couldn't make that the headline, of course. Dr. Zhang hadn't published her calculations. We couldn't risk our credibility. Then again—as multiple coworkers vented to me—Dr. Zhang *was* a credible source. It was frustrating. We were about to get beaten to history by the grocery store tabloid aisle.

After an hour of pitches and one shattered coffee mug, the managing editor settled on my draft: *Prototype for Interstellar Travel Complete, Says Renowned Physicist.*

It was honest. Not too flashy. Journalists aren't supposed to make promises we can't support. Our responsibility is to the truth, not dreams. The public deserves the truth.

* * *

Kids deserve to dream.

"When we go to space, where do you want to visit first?" Jade tugged the sheets to her chin.

I pretended to think. "Let's go to Titan. Surface oceans and fourteen percent gravity. The perfect vacation spot."

That earned me the eye roll I was expecting. "You can't surf on Titan, Dad. They're hydrocarbon lakes, not oceans. It's not dense enough. You'd just sink."

"Oh. Silly me." Outer space was one topic I did not have to feign any ignorance on. "What about you?"

"I can't tell you," her face was deadly serious, "because I'm going to an undiscovered planet. I think I'll name it *Shiva*."

"Wow. You've got this all figured out, haven't you?"

"Maybe not the name. But all the other planets are named after Roman gods, and that's not very fair."

"How about *Ma'at*," I offered, "the goddess of truth and

justice."

Jade looked at me pityingly, like I was the child who needed explaining to. "But I already *have* a backup name," she insisted, "Planet Bobby."

Bobby was her pet hamster's name.

I chuckled and kissed her forehead. "I'm sure you can discover two planets, sunshine."

* * *

"She's got nothing!" my boss roared. "Nada! Zilch!"

"We didn't *say* she had anything," I massaged my temples, "just that she *claimed* to have something. I'll report the leak, okay...?"

I stared at the blank document for long enough that my coffee got cold. Finally, I managed to type a headline. *NASA Leak Proves Interstellar Travel Claims Fraudulent.* I stared at the words until they were just black shapes on a screen. Then I made a correction. *NASA Leak Suggests...*

Next, there was the question of why she did it. Everyone at work had their own theory. It fell to me to copyedit them into something usable. I came across more than one contemporary paraphrase of "female hysteria."

* * *

With Jade at school, the house was empty. I used to walk the dog when I needed to get outside. But Scout was dead. I wandered down the sidewalk without an excuse. That year, it was easy to pick out the newly gentrified streets. I only had to look for which trees weren't crawling with cicadas, trees that hadn't been here seventeen years ago.

I watched the tiny marvels squirm from the mulch. *Beautiful things from the earth as well.* The nymphs emerge with vigor. Only a month to breed, only a month, breed breed breed, they thought. *They don't need to know about the stars.*

* * *

April 13th. It would go down in history as the day when... well, *April 13th* happened. No explanation needed. *July 4th. September 11th. April 13th.*

"It's a fake. It's a hack, or a... photo-chop or something."

"Photoshop."

"Whatever. It's a hoax. Do *not* report on this."

I looked back at my monitor, at the same compressed JPEG that was probably loaded on every screen in the world. Rolling red hills. A landscape that, by appearances, could have been from Earth, but of course, that would be impossible. Visible plainly in the Martian soil, footprints spelled a phrase now overwhelming the servers of Google Translate: *Quod erat demonstrandum.* Translation: *believe me now?*

* * *

The FBI found her on a ranch in Wyoming. No spaceship, no magic gateway. Just her, a woman in a lab coat. A podcaster started a theory that Dr. Zhang somehow used the Mars rover itself to write the message—*She's some kind of genius, isn't she? Like, a hacker genius?* The accusation trended for several hours until the internet collectively realized that rovers don't have feet.

It was a striking front-page photo. A pile of shredded paper and scorched motherboards. During interrogation, reportedly, Dr. Zhang smugly informed the investigators that there was still one type of memory drive their technology could not search.

But not even the constraints of reality can stop a Congressional subpoena. Congress opened an investigation into

Dr. Zhang's "destruction of government property" under Title 18, US Code § 1361, and article eight of the Outer Space Treaty.

That's what I had to write. The facts. If you really wanted to know what Kamilah Zhang was on trial for, you just had to check social media. Everyone was arguing the same question.

If she had the technology, why didn't she share it?

People fell into three camps. The first declared the April 13th phenomenon a hoax. The second, that Dr. Zhang was extorting the US Government. The third camp declared everything else, ranging from something about alien body snatchers to the sinister machinations of a particular ex-secretary of state.

There was really no point in theorizing. You could just wait for the Congressional Record to release their transcripts.

* * *

The Senate Subcommittee on Commerce, Justice, Science, and Related Agencies was ready to convene the moment Kamilah Zhang touched down in Washington. Congress even came out of recess for the occasion. Senator Huxley presided.

When it came time for her to speak, Kamilah Zhang leaned almost imperceptibly closer to the microphone. "The data from my laboratory are considered records. I made the decision not to refer them to the Aeronautics and Space Administration."

"So you willfully disregarded your duty," Senator Huxley continued, "your... *sacred* duty, which you swore to uphold—"

"That's where we disagree," Dr. Zhang interrupted. "Oppenheimer fulfilled his duty on paper, but what about his duty to the world? Of course," she said, beginning to lean away from the microphone, "of course, he owed his superiors answers. But he could have drawn out the search. Keep them looking into heavy water, for example... buy time for a peaceful end."

A remarkably optimistic view. But that wasn't what Senator Huxley took issue with.

"Destroying government records is treason."

"Please. Some decorum," Senator Hart spoke up. Blue pantsuit. Third in line for the Democratic nomination. "Look, Dr. Zhang. I understand. Here you are," she emphasized with a squint, "with the power to change history."

"I don't want to be Oppenheimer—"

"—and responsibility can be awfully stressful—"

"—I want to be Frederick Banting."

A pause of confusion turned into real silence as Dr. Zhang drew herself up. "Banting. The man who sold the patent of insulin for one dollar, who ensured that his research would save lives rather than generate profit."

"Then follow his example," Senator Hart insisted, "share your research."

"Insulin today costs $360.25 per month," Dr. Zhang replied. "This economy didn't deserve Banting's trust. It will have to earn mine."

"Dr. Zhang," Senator Huxley interjected, "have you had any affiliation with the Communist Party of China?"

"Mister Senator, I think I've made very clear my position on any such profit-driven entities." Kamilah wouldn't let him goad her into producing any sound bites. "Look. I am willing to disclose some details from my research. They are necessary details to understand my decision."

The room quieted.

"The technology that I have developed can transport matter anywhere in the universe. Senator Hart, imagine what could be done with that kind of capability..."

"We could have clean energy, better waste management—"

"I agree. We could have benefits for all mankind, which is to say—not profits. But is that what Amazon and Exxon-Mobil will think of, Senator? How will you respond when corporations start hosting off-world fulfillment centers far, far away from US jurisdiction?"

The Congressional Record doesn't include air quotes in its transcripts. You'll have to guess where she put them.

"The federal government exists to regulate private industry, Dr. Zhang," Senator Hart said. "It exists to address these very concerns."

"With all due respect, Senator. The purpose of a machine is what we use it for."

* * *

When the FBI took Dr. Zhang into custody, the editorial board called it an "unprecedented breach of judicial norms." They imprisoned her so that she couldn't give her discovery to any foreign governments. That's what we were saying.

I was assigned to write a piece reminding everyone to be very concerned about precedents. Even if you didn't agree with Dr. Zhang, her civil liberties were our own.

It needed to be said.

I would leave it for someone else to say. I decided to call out of work.

* * *

I was on another walk when I heard something hiss beneath me. A cicada helpless on the concrete, its broken legs waggling in the air.

Normally, I'd squash it. Call it a mercy killing. I stared down at the concrete.

We didn't have to be trapped here. There was someone who could help us. *Someone too busy arguing with millionaires on C-SPAN*, I fumed.

The newsroom and the editorial board hadn't been on speaking terms since the announcement. But it was the only thing I had the energy to write.

OPINION: Kamilah Zhang Thinks Her Politics Are the Center of the Universe. She's Wrong.

* * *

I was expecting my coworkers to be angry. It was only fair. Who knew how many hate messages had been lobbed at them because of what I wrote?

What I wasn't expecting was for my boss to walk in with a buddy-buddy smile plastered across his face. I furrowed my brow.

"*Great* timing. Really had your finger on the pulse for this one."

I didn't understand his sarcasm until he dropped an early draft of today's front page on my desk.

Dr. Kamilah Zhang Dead of Apparent Suicide in Federal Custody.

"Good luck out there, Krish. You'll need it."

* * *

Someone had to drive Jade to school. I tried to ignore the scathing looks. A few days ago, all these PTA parents in their smart watches and yoga pants had silently agreed with me. But that wouldn't show up if you googled their names. Not like my op-ed.

I had it out for her all along. That's what social media thought. Why else had I refused to report on Dr. Zhang between the first announcement and her death?

I started taking my walks late at night when the streets were empty. I slept while Jade was at school. I didn't have to worry about work since quitting, but I still couldn't escape the endless theorizing of my coworkers.

If they couldn't have the technology, nobody could. So they killed her.

No, they're dissecting her brain to figure it out. That's why we haven't seen the body.

I couldn't speculate. Only one question consumed my nightly walks.

Why did she tell us if she knew we couldn't meet her demands?

Guilt gnawed at me. A woman was dead, and I was mourning her research.

* * *

"What's that?" I pointed at the piece of poster board in Jade's hands as she climbed into the backseat of the minivan.

She turned it around. *Galileo* was written in bubble letters across the top.

"Nice! Are you gonna study space someday, like he did...?"

"Maybe," she replied glumly. "Ms. Kleinman said it was too late to change my presentation topic."

"Oh. Okay."

* * *

Once Jade was in bed, I flipped open my laptop.

It was just a school project. But it reminded me of something that I couldn't name. It was on the tip of my tongue. My fingers hovered over the keyboard. I typed the only thing that ever crossed my mind when it was otherwise blank.

Kamilah Zhang.

42,800,000 results. My cursor hovered over the video thumbnail.

Click.

"It's done," her voice came through the speakers.

Click. Muted.

I didn't want to listen, to fool myself into thinking she was there and talking to me. That would mean I could apologize. I looked at the wall behind her. Something had been strange about the poster. Now I saw what. Earth was at the center, surrounded by concentric gold rings.

Galileo would go down in history for defending heliocentrism until he died, imprisoned for heresy. Religion versus science. The passion of Christ versus the passion for truth. Martyr versus martyr. I stared at the poster behind Dr. Zhang.

It was a message. A time capsule.

Everyone liked to imagine that they would side with Galileo. Especially journalists. After all, our first duty was to truth, even if we don't like where it leads. Or the enemies it leads us to.

* * *

Jade asked if she could stay up past her bedtime to join me on my nightly walk.

"Wait up!" she called out a few meters behind me. She was on her hands and knees, parsing through the wet grass.

"What are you doing?"

"Looking for bugs. New ones. There could be a brand-new kind of bug right here! I read that over eight hundred insect species are discovered every year."

I didn't even think about correcting her. Kids deserve to dream. I nodded along, half-listening.

"Bugs bugs bugs bugs bugs."

I stared at the tree trunks, covered with the translucent, amber carapaces where cicadas had crawled from their exoskeletons.

I stared at the empty husks and frowned. They leave behind their old bodies. They do not hold onto old weight to fly...

We never saw her body.

* * *

This story first appeared in the After Dinner Conversation—August 2023 issue.

Discussion Questions

1. The narrator (*Krish*) says, "Everyone liked to imagine that they would side with Galileo." What does this mean? Why would people side against new science? Why might you side with, or against, Galileo (*or Dr. Zhang*)?

2. What do you think are the ramifications of Dr. Zhang's discovery, assuming it is true? Do you think it would be a net positive, or negative, for humanity?

3. Why do you think Dr. Zhang wanted to prove her discovery to the world only to deny providing it? If you were in her situation, what would you do? Do you think an inventor who withholds world-changing technology deserves civil liberties, or do the needs of the many outweigh one individual's liberties?

4. If you had a world-changing discovery that you wanted to guarantee would get out into the world in the most nonprofit-driven way, how would you do it? Under what, if any, circumstances should a world-changing discovery be driven by profit motives?

5. What do you think happened to Dr. Zhang?

* * *

The Things We Give

Allison Padron

* * *

<u>**Content Disclosure**</u>: Strong Language; Depiction of Alcohol Use

* * *

The Collection Specialist at LifeCorp has no softness to her. Everything about her is a razor's edge—her sleek black ponytail, needlepoint stilettos, bony elbows, and long fingers. She smiles without any real kindness as she sits across from the woman in the ratty sweater and dirty sneakers.

"Can I have your full name, ma'am?" The specialist's fingers sweep across the thin white keyboard in front of her.

"Martha Johnson."

"Thank you." The woman's blue eyes drop to peer through the glass table, watching Martha's left leg bounce. "Now, Ms. Johnson, before we approve you for the procedure, I need to ask you a few questions. Is that alright with you?"

Martha's brow lifts slightly. Then she nods, brown eyes flicking from side to side as she takes in the room again.

Gleaming white walls, a floor so polished she can see her reflection. It's all perfect, sterile, unfeeling.

The specialist smiles again, revealing prominent incisors. "Fantastic. What's your occupation?"

"I'm a waitress. Over at The Golden Biscuit."

The keys make tiny clicks as the woman types, the only sound in the windowless room. "What's your estimated annual salary? Tips included."

"I reckon that's my fucking business."

The specialist stops moving. She looks back to Martha. Her eyes never seem to blink. "Of course, you're welcome to keep it confidential, Ms. Johnson, but we can't proceed without that information."

Martha clenches and unclenches her jaw before she speaks. "About $25,000."

"Thank you, Ms. Jo—"

"Jesus, quit doing that. Just call me Martha."

The specialist finally blinks before smiling. It's a patronizing smile like she's speaking to an insolent child. "Of course, Martha. My apologies. So, $25,000 a year. Do you drink or smoke?"

"All of the above."

"How frequently?"

"A pack a day and a few beers at night."

"Do you exercise?"

"No."

"Any children?"

"No."

"Do you travel?"

"No. Unless you count commuting."

The specialist finishes typing. "Thank you, Martha. That's all the personal information we'll need—though we will require you to verify your income before we proceed." The soulless smile returns. "We should discuss the procedure and your preferred method of compensation. How many years were you interested in selling?"

"I was thinking just one."

"Just one." The specialist nods, glancing over at her computer screen. "For one year, we can give you $20,000. Would you like us to—"

"Wait—wait just a fucking minute, lady. $20,000? Are you fucking with me?"

Bemused eyes meet Martha's, and for a second, the other woman seems unsure how to react. "I don't understand your question, Ms. Johnson."

"My friend's husband got $500,000 for one year. That's the whole reason I came in here—to sell a year and be set!"

"What does your friend's husband do for a living?"

"He's a surgeon. Heart or brain or something like that."

The specialist smiles. "Oh! I see. This is just a simple misunderstanding, Ms. Johnson."

"Martha."

"Right. You see, there's not a flat price per year. It varies from person to person based on salary and various additional life factors."

Martha's leg bounces even faster. "That doesn't make any damn sense. A year's a year, isn't it? The billionaires are getting the same number of days no matter the source."

That insufferable smile grows even wider, ever more patient. "We aren't paying for the year, per se, but instead reimbursing you for giving up a year of *your* life. Therefore, we take all factors into consideration to determine what one year in your life is worth, and then we compensate every person fairly."

Martha's eye twitches, her fingers drumming against her stationary leg. It takes her a few moments to compose herself before she speaks. "That won't work. I need... well, I need $350,000."

"In that case, you can sell eighteen years and have money to spare."

A choked sound erupts from Martha's throat. "*Eighteen years?*"

"If you want $350,000."

She stands suddenly, knocking the chair back a few inches. "I can't do this."

The specialist stands as well, frowning for the first time. "Of course, it's your choice, Martha. If you change your mind, you know where to find us."

The squeak of Martha's dirty sneakers on the shining floor is her only response.

* * *

Her shift that afternoon is dogshit. It ends with twenty in cash and an insulting lack of tips. She blows the cash at the bar down the street and is lucky enough to score a few free beers off a man in a leather jacket.

That night she calls Benito.

"Can you believe it, Benny? $20,000 for a year of my life? Is that all I'm worth?" Martha steadies herself on the concrete wall outside the bar, her words slurring together.

"I can believe it, babe. You're hardly the Queen of England."

"Shut up, asshole." The world around her spins, a bad sign. She leans forward a little, and the nausea overtakes her, spilling vomit onto the pavement at her feet.

A group of college boys are walking out of the bar at that moment. She can hear their laughter. "Go home, you old coot," one of them calls, and the rest snicker.

Benny clears his throat, and the reception crackles. "I told you not to go to LifeCorp. They're a bunch of soul suckers."

Martha rubs her throbbing forehead. "I don't think I have much of a choice anymore."

"You gotta do what you think is best. Hey—are you out? You should come over."

"You only want me to come over when I'm drunk."

"You only bother to call me when you've been drinking."

"Touché." With the taste of vomit lingering on her tongue, she looks up at the fluorescent lights of the corner store. "Fine. I'm coming. Just let me grab a bottle of water first." Martha hangs up without waiting for a response.

* * *

The next week, Martha walks through the front door of LifeCorp again, hands stuffed in her sweatshirt pocket. The blade-thin specialist smiles at her from behind the desk. "Ms. John—Martha. It's good to see you. I saw that you submitted the tax forms. Have you—"

"Let's just get this over with," Martha snaps, pushing past her into the hallway. The click of heels from behind grates on her nerves, but she keeps her composure. Barely.

The specialist sinks into the chair behind the desk. "Would you still like to sell one year?"

"I'll do eighteen." Martha's leg starts bouncing again, and

she instinctively reaches for the cigarette pack in her pocket before realizing they probably don't allow smoking in here. Figures.

That smile grows wider, sharper, and the keyboard clicks as she types. "Eighteen years. That'll be $360,000. Do you prefer electronic transfer or check?"

"A check is fine."

With a nod and a few more clicks, the specialist ends the pre-procedure meeting. Martha is escorted down the hallway to a dim room with an exam chair in the middle of the barren space. The specialist tells her to sit, and then she starts pulling out needles and tubes from the drawers below the computer.

"You're going to stick me?" Martha asks, feeling like a caged animal.

The woman smiles again, her blue eyes locking onto Martha's brown ones. "Only in a few spots. And the needles are so thin that you won't feel a thing."

"How long have you been doing this, anyway?" Martha shifts in the seat, trying to get comfortable. The specialist is right—she can't feel the first needle even when it slides into her wrist.

The specialist moves to the other wrist, then both her ankles. "Since LifeCorp opened their first public clinic. So... nearly ten years. I've seen countless patients, so don't worry. You're in good hands."

A faint glow from the screen next to the chair illuminates the specialist's face as she puts the final needle in the base of Martha's throat.

Martha closes her eyes, inhaling deeply. "Will this hurt?"

A few clicks and a mechanical humming sound. Martha

hears the specialist drumming on the keyboard again. "Don't worry about that. You won't even know it's happening." The specialist is right. Martha doesn't feel any different when she leaves a half hour later, check in hand.

* * *

The first place Martha goes is the bank. After that, she goes back to the bar. She's got an extra $10,000 to do with as she pleases, and she wants to get obliterated.

The next morning, nursing a hangover, she writes out checks and mails them. Then she drives to the nursing home. The receptionist greets her with an overly warm smile. "Martha! Miss Betty is in her room. I'm sure she'll be glad to see you."

"Thanks, Anita," Martha says, taking two peppermints from the jar on the desk and heading down the familiar corridors.

Betty is sitting in the chair by the window, watching the birds at the garden feeder. Her roommate isn't there, which Martha is grateful for; the woman has a staring problem.

"Hey, Mom," Martha says gently, settling into the chair on the other side of the table. "I brought you a peppermint."

Betty glances between her daughter and the candy, smiling slowly as she takes it from her hand. "What a nice girl you are. Would you like to stay for dinner?"

Martha forces a smile, resting her chin on her hand. "No, thank you. It's a little early for dinner, and I have work at four."

Betty purses her lips, then looks out the window again, hand clenched tightly around the plastic wrapper. Martha reaches over, takes the peppermint back, and opens the packaging. "Mom, you need to actually put it in your mouth to eat it."

"A nice, nice girl," Betty responds, popping the peppermint in her mouth. It rattles between her teeth for a while. Martha puts her own candy in her mouth and watches the sparrows.

After a bit, she clears her throat. "I want you to know I sent in the money for Dad's bills. All of them—hospital and funeral. So you don't have to worry."

Martha keeps staring out the window. She can feel her mother's blank gaze on her cheek, but she can't bear to meet it. They sit like that for several moments before Betty smiles. "Would you like some dinner?"

A soft exhale escapes Martha's mouth, and she buries her face in her hands. After a moment, she stands, pushing away from the table. "I'll be back in a few days, Mom. Don't forget to take your medication." It's a useless parting phrase, but she says it every time, like a bad habit.

Martha has already closed the door behind her, ignoring Betty's cheerful "Goodbye!", when the nurse places a gentle hand on her arm.

"I was about to bring her lunch in, and I couldn't help but overhear... It's a great thing you've done, but it's no use telling her about it. It might upset her, you know, to remember her husband. Even for a few seconds. Her memory is getting pretty short these days."

The muscles in Martha's jaw clench. "Yeah, I gathered that. Thanks." She wrenches her arm away and heads back out to her car, wiping the moisture from her eyes with a rough hand.

* * *

That night, Martha chain smokes. Then she calls Benito.

* * *

Life goes on. For a while, everything is fine. Back to normal. She makes enough to pay for rent and gas and a shit ton of beer. Sometimes she goes to Benny's.

Until those two pink lines divide her world in half.

Martha has to smoke through most of a cigarette pack before she can think about that little white test. She'd chug a handle of vodka if she could to help make sense of it. The only thing she can think to do is call Benito.

He hangs up on her. Martha throws her phone at the wall and lies face down on the couch until her doorbell rings. When she answers the door, Benito is standing there. He pulls her into his arms, catching her off guard. She sobs against his chest for the better part of an hour.

When she's calmed down, he orders Chinese food, and they sit on the rickety balcony.

"I don't have any savings, Benny. I can barely afford rent." She whispers into the twilight haze, her eyes still throbbing from her tears.

He stares down at his fried rice. "We'll move in together. Then we have two jobs and only one rent payment."

"Will it be enough?"

Benito is silent for a long moment, and Martha's leg starts to bounce. Then he clears his throat. "We could each give a year. I wager I'm worth about $30,000—together, that's $50,000. That's a good start, right?"

Martha buries her head in her hands. "Okay," she whispers, heart in her throat. That would be nineteen years gone. Leaving her with, what, fifteen years or so? It's bleak, but Martha's used to bleak. Besides, they're out of options.

But she's used to that, too.

* * *

They go in together, but Martha has to sit in the waiting room while Benito goes with the specialist. After twenty minutes, he reemerges, giving her a weak smile. "$35,000. Better than we expected."

He sits in the chair while she heads to the back. They skip the meeting this time since the company already has all her information. The needles slide in, one at a time. Martha watches the shadows on the ceiling in the half-light.

"Another year this time, Martha?" The specialist's black ponytail sways as she stands up and moves to the computer.

"Yeah."

There are a few clicks, a whir, and then a beep. The specialist blinks at the computer, then at Martha. "Can you confirm your age for me?"

"I'm thirty-seven." Martha sits up slightly, frowning at the back of the monitor. "Why?"

A smile. "Let me just check something in the program." A few clicks, a whir, and a beep again.

The specialist lets out an exhale, walking back to Martha's side and pulling out the needles. "I'm sorry, Ms. Johnson, but you're no longer eligible for this procedure," she says pleasantly.

Martha stares at her. "Why? Is it because I'm pregnant?"

"No."

"Then why?"

The woman clears her throat delicately. "You're attempting to donate more time than is left in your lifespan."

Martha's heart stutters a *one-two* in her chest. It feels like it stops.

It was just one year. A single year. She doesn't even have

a year left? Her hands curl in and out of fists, and her mouth goes painfully dry. "That can't be right."

"I assure you the program has never had an error."

"Well, it must have had one now. Check again."

The specialist sighs. "I'm sorry, Ms. Johnson. I checked multiple times. You have my deepest condolen—"

Something inside of Martha snaps. She leaps out of the chair, wrapping her hands around the specialist's throat and slamming her into the wall. "Check again!" She spits, hysteria crawling through her chest. "That can't be right! You're lying. *You're making shit up!*"

"Get your hands off of me." The specialist's expression has soured, her lip curling in disgust.

"You stole *eighteen* years of my life!" Martha screams, shaking her. The specialist knees her in the groin and steps aside as Martha folds in half. She presses a button on the wall and turns back to the weeping woman.

"You sold us those years of your own volition," the specialist says coldly, dusting off the front of her dress. "It's not our fault if you smoked and drank your lifespan down beforehand."

Martha straightens and lunges, but she's intercepted. A large man has come in through the doorway, summoned by the call of the button. He tucks her arms behind her back, holding her still as she thrashes.

"Take her out through the back," the specialist says, reaching up to readjust her ponytail. "I have another client coming in the front soon."

The man starts toward the back of the room, and Martha sobs. "Wait—please, wait!" The specialist signals, and the man stops. Martha takes a few hitched breaths, bent over the man's large forearm. Her blurred gaze turns to the specialist, pleading with her. "What... What am I supposed to do? What do I do now?"

The specialist smiles broadly and tilts her head. "If you want my professional opinion, Ms. Johnson, I'd suggest booking a pregnancy termination. There's a great clinic just down the street. After that, you can spend your final few months the way you spent the rest of your life—drunk and useless."

Martha breaks down. She's still sobbing when the back door is locked behind her.

* * *

This story first appeared in the After Dinner Conversation—July 2023 issue.

Discussion Questions

1. If you could sell years off the end of your life, would you? If so, how many years would you sell and for what price?

2. Do you agree with Martha selling eighteen years off the end of her life to pay for her dead father's bills and her mother's care? Should she simply have left her parents to financially fend for themselves?

3. At the end of the story, the specialist tells Martha she is "drunk and useless." While this is certainly a cruel thing to tell someone, is it inaccurate as well? Is Martha drunk and useless to society?

4. Is there a difference between selling years of your life for money versus selling years of your life to a job for money? What, if anything, is the difference in the time for money exchanges?

5. Is there anything inherently wrong with spending your life drinking, socializing, and generally being unfocused on future goals? Is this an accurate description of Martha, or is there something else going on?

* * *

Two-Percenters

CJ Erick

* * *

Content Disclosure: Mild Language; Suicidal Themes; Low
Intensity; Death or Bereavement

* * *

Reginah stared at the crystal vial her friend Twylea had
laid on her desk. A gentle light bloomed within the desk's frosty
surface, illuminating the liquid sealed in the vial in shades of
lavender.

"Go on," she prompted. Twylea could be annoyingly slow
in disclosing useful context.

Reginah's friend, like all Socials, was divine-like in beauty,
carved from alabaster and gold. Every pose, tiniest movement,
or inflection in her voice was precisely tuned to thrill and
disarm the observer. Even knowing this, Reginah often fell
under her friend's spell. And today Twylea bore a gift.

"Imagine if you will," Twylea said, in the purr of a femme
fatale, "a world where everyone could be a Two-Percenter."

Twylea was also intentionally vague, which she knew was

frustrating for Rationals like Reginah. And she knew Reginah hated the commoners' label for her kind. It demeaned the Gifted's genetic superiority.

"That's been studied by hundreds of researchers," Reginah said. "The physiological and genetic inhibitions for those in the general population have never been successfully overcome. At least ten million commoners have died or been disfigured attempting it." She purposefully ignored the pretty ornament. "The council sponsors continue the research, but the consensus is it will never be done. Discussing it further is pointless fantasy."

Even for a "Two-Percenter," a genetically enhanced humanoid, Twylea was a stunning wonder, with enhancements focused on outward beauty, voice, posture, emotional expression. The perfect host, actor, debate panelist, politician. Inches taller than Reginah at nearly two full meters, body fit and toned with little or no work and built along Vitruvian mathematical proportions; flawless skin and golden hair framing her perfect heart-shaped face; eyes the color of the vial's lavender liquid, the color of wisdom, royalty, and first love; lips and cheeks and ears mathematically perfect; chameleon skin tone adapting to ambient light, mood, and purpose. Cleopatra or Helen or Aphrodite would pale in comparison.

Twylea's pianist's fingers tipped across the desk, and the inner light from the desk's surface sparkled from her golden nails. Her fingers stopped inches away and retreated. "Humor me for a minute." Reginah found she could do nothing else. "How many of us are there?"

"Here in the North American Region? Two per million.

About one thousand. Worldwide—twenty thousand."

"How would you describe our influence?"

Reginah shook herself to clear her head. "Your Socratic method is annoying. Get to the point." But Twylea just smiled. "Fine, I'll play."

Twylea's eyes twinkled. "Of course you will."

"Influence? We've been the driving force behind nearly every recent advancement—science, mathematics, physics, art... politics." She nodded toward Twylea as she spoke the last.

"For how long?"

"You know this, since 2045, when Orinheim and Hatomi perfected their recombinant techniques."

"And how far have we come in the last fifty years as a species?"

"Since the first hundred were identified and enhanced, trifold acceleration. Even our best statisticians struggle to define the rate of advancement. We continue to surpass the models."

Twylea smiled in approval, but it seemed bloodless, now that Reginah had withdrawn from her spell. Even her Social persona could not hide her inner tension from Reginah's Rational inspection.

"Yes. So imagine where we could go if all people could undergo the enhancements and not just the lucky few. Anything would be possible, perhaps even a final, complete understanding of the universe."

"Or total chaos, reminiscent of the Dark Ages. In the current structure, we lead progress, commerce, governance, albeit through shadow influence. There is no war, no poverty, little disease and that cured in weeks rather than years. The commoners recognize our superiority, if reminded gently on occasion, and we maintain order. But make us all relatively equal again—it could all break down. Or become obsolete. We just don't know."

Reginah cursed her friend silently, for wasting her time speculating worthless scenarios. It distracted from the work; twisted her mind in knots. "Either way, it would be 'Utopia,' in the Greek origins of the word—'No place.'—because it's never going to happen."

Twylea had let her disarming smile fall, something she seldom did. She bit her lip, something she never did.

"Do you think our privilege is fair?"

Reginah felt her friend's tension spread to her own thoughts. Why would Twylea push this question to her, a Rational? She wanted a Judicial, or a Sophist. Gratefully, she let Reginah off the hook and answered her own question.

"I don't," said Twylea. "For thousands of years, people have dreamed of gods coming from the sky to guide them, or feared others coming to make them pets."

"I know where you're going. We are not pet masters. Or puppeteers."

"We feed them. We keep water in their bowls, and even develop better ways to scoop their waste. And by not working to repair this imbalance, we sentence them to staying in their yards."

"At best, we are driving the new awakening. At worst, they live in pretty nice yards."

Twylea's smile didn't return, but her eyes turned their full mesmerizing power on Reginah. She pushed the vial inches forward with a finger so well shaped it resembled a ballet dancer's leg.

Reginah asked, "Is this a new deodorant for the yards?"

"You're very snide for a Rational. No, darling, this is the magic potion that turns all the pets into gods."

Twylea paused, expecting Reginah to provide the echo. "How?"

"Orinheim. He gave it to me before he... died." Dr. Benjamin Orinheim was the esteemed Rational presiding over the Bureau of Genetic Development, the agency through which all enhancements were orchestrated. Even among the Gifted, his name was spoken in hushed tones. *A god among gods*, she thought, then crushed it immediately. He'd died months earlier in a rare lab accident while repairing one of his gene-painting machines.

"Why did he spend his precious research time working on this problem?"

"Introspection. Regret, I think."

"Why did he give it to you?"

"He trusted me. I was selected to be one of his consorts."

"That bastard."

"No, I applied. This was Orinheim, Reginah. It made no sense for him to spend time pursuing relationships. But he still had personal needs."

"Maybe he should have 'enhanced' those away. And I'm not buying the regret explanation. He didn't create the rules that favor us. Why should he feel guilty to be Gifted?"

Twylea settled back into the formless ergo lounge, suddenly looking very human and very tired, like a five-a.m. harlot.

"I said regret, not guilt. He asked me to run an underground team to gather reports on the long-term effects of the growing class divide. Our findings were not encouraging."

"He carried on research without Institute sanction?"

Twylea's eyes twinkled again. "You would be surprised by what influence can accomplish, even in Valhalla. What Orinheim wanted, he pursued."

It was Reginah's turn to sit back and feel tired. There was something very odd and yet suspiciously familiar about Twylea bringing the token and its story to her.

Twylea went on. "The edges are already starting to fray. The latest executive reports show more crime in nearly every district. Even violent crime, for the first time in 25 years, despite nearly universal surveillance and rapid response. Anti-government protests are growing in all seven continental regions. Psychosis, depression, suicide, all on the rise. And all of this supports our findings that things are not going well."

"And Dr. O's response was to make us all equal again, introducing a new age of unrestrained materialism, war, and class stratification beyond anything our best models can predict."

"Possibly. But no pets. No yards. No genetic lottery. No technological injustice."

"Just all the other really fine types of injustice. So why bring this to me? You have 'the cure.' Dr. O and his disciples believed this is the right thing to do. Why not release it to the world? Bring the New Age. Be heroes."

"His death wasn't an accident." Twylea's jaw was set, and her eyes drawn down, like Athena after she'd wet herself. "He couldn't live with himself not using it."

Reginah decided to wait her out this time, as long as it took. Meanwhile, part of her mind processed everything her friend had offered. The neural communications implant in her cortex accessed the Institute's Date and Records Library, and she reviewed the studies Twylea had referenced. Searching for an academic dagger, Reginah found none, no inconsistencies in Twylea's story. Of course, the foundation of her revelation, the secret studies and production of the contents of the vial, couldn't be corroborated, nor could she find any mention or rumor of them. So, none of it could be debunked.

Twylea sat forward again, eyeing the vial. "It adds a peptide sequence on three different chromosomes that simulate the family of genes that allow us to undergo enhancement therapy. Within weeks, most commoners can begin the enhancement treatments."

Reginah zoomed her eyes in, searching for telltales of molecular magic suspended in the liquid. But the genetic machinery, if it was there as Twylea said, was too elusory for even her enhanced vision. She shifted her spectrum further into the UV range, and the vial seemed to flare with neon fire. But it held its secrets, just colored liquid rocking in the faceted glass.

"So Dr. O solved the problem that a thousand studies couldn't."

"Yes." That, simply.

"The proof?"

"Thomas Belton."

"The late bloomer? I thought his parents raised him in a Regressive sect, and he was discovered late."

Belton had emerged in his mid-thirties, long after most Gifted were placed in the program. He had advanced quickly, now a Commercist, leading one of the three North American regional banks in Sacramento. Like most of the Gifted, Reginah had been identified at the age of seven during standardized testing, and her most suitable specialty gleaned over the next two years.

Twylea shook her head, a negative gesture that had crushed men's hearts.

"He was born a commoner. He applied for the research study, and Dr. Orinheim chose him for his age and demographic, and because his sect ties provided the perfect explanation. The transition took two years. There were others, many successful, but Dr. Belton the most so."

"So why hasn't this crossed over from the subjects to others?"

"The gene splicing is stable, and needs a vector." She nodded at the vial, but seemed to avoid touching it. "Dr. Orinheim chose a rhinovirus. The recipient develops a case of the sniffles, no more." She eyed the vial now with something like unhappiness. "And then they join us."

Reginah felt a safety valve about to pop, threatening to blow her annoyance all over the room.

"You're looking at that thing like it's a poisonous snake and not the healing elixir for all humanity's woes. There's a downside, obviously. Spill it, or stop wasting my time."

Twylea's frown deepened, and Reginah had to fight the urge to hug her. Her friend's voice dropped like a funeral recitation.

"It changes us also." And that, simply.

Reginah stifled a laugh. She'd at last deduced the real intention of this meeting. Twylea was conducting a psychology experiment, and Reginah was the subject.

"So I'm guessing we don't become double-gifted."

"No. At best, our enhancements are rejected over time, and we become... common, as you would say. Worse—debilitating handicaps. Worst—grotesque disfiguration and painful death." Her eyes swung up to meet Reginah's, and oh the act was excellent, award-worthy. A single tear gathered in Twylea's azure sea of an eye. "Socials suffer the most."

"How do you know this?"

"Dr. Orinheim modeled it, tried to eliminate the rejection. There were trials..." The tear she'd been nurturing slid down her cheek, like a fake glass pearl.

"Why me?" On the surface, her question meant why give Reginah the vial, but beneath that, why choose her for the study? Even as she thought this, a bristling pang of doubt pricked her mind. Damn Twylea and her agenda. Even Reginah's powers of logic and rationale couldn't protect her from the psychological hooks.

"Who else but a Rational, and who else among them but someone I can trust? Please don't hate me. I can't let it loose. I can't let it... I just can't. My niece, Freesia, a Social like me. I know it's the right thing—for the most people, for the future of our species—but I can't do this to MY people." She slumped, seemed to shrink into the body of a young girl, the person she had been before genetic magic had metamorphosed her into a goddess. "Please don't hate me."

As suddenly as a light going out, she rose and left the office. Left behind was the MacGuffin, the vial of colored liquid possessing incredible power. Or none.

After Twylea's after-image faded in Reginah's mind, she settled back in her chair, pushed herself down into a meditative state, and spoke the word that would trigger her mind into a deep trance.

"Spinneret."

Her mental processes divided into isolated silos. Her persona, formerly called the "ego," stood aside much like a spectator at a sporting event, and she observed her logic center dissecting the inputs from Twylea's visit. She evaluated each of Twylea's assertions independently, categorized and filed them, and assigned multi-variable Monte Carlo probability curves to each. She then modeled a spectrum of systems, manipulating the individual assertions in hierarchical indices of weighted average relevance. Her communication portal again accessed the Institute's library to review relevant information in the databases. After these models processed the data to a resolution of initial findings, she adjusted those conclusions by analyzing Twylea's behavior, mood choices, and emotional expression. The algorithms churned for what seemed like hours, but when the processes were complete, she rose from the trance to find that only six minutes had passed.

With a certainty of 93.6 percent, she concluded that she had in fact been enrolled in a psychological experiment, with a similar certainty that her reaction and response would affect her future opportunities and career track. If it was a test, the vial contained only colored water, and the correct response was to smash it on a crowded walkway to simulate releasing the virus.

The most interesting aspect was that if Twylea's assertions were true and the vial contained genetic transformation, then the correct response was the same. The benefit of the many superseded the penalties for the few.

She needed a walk anyway.

She scooped the vial into her tunic pocket, took the tube

down to ground level, then pushed through the building's security field and onto the softwalk. The crush of commoners on the walk spread away from her, giving her more than ample personal space as she melded into their flow, some nodding or tipping their sloped hats, most avoiding eye contact. The Institute discouraged special treatment for the Gifted, either deferential or negative, but their efforts were largely unsuccessful. The Gifted would never fit into common society any more than she could step onto this softwalk without causing ripples.

Likely under surveillance, she moved with the tortoise-like flow along the walk, stifling her inclination to press through them. The city was served by several modes of aerial and subterranean public transit, bullet tubes and sky buses, and many private options. And yet the press of walking humanity never lessened, as if there was an informal prohibition against modernity. The influence of fringe anti-progressive cults couldn't account for it.

Judging from the lack of fitness of the people near her and avoiding her attention, most of them weren't walking for exercise. Her nose informed that hygiene was also not a priority even in the summer heat. She could smell their disease and age and injury and addiction, in an effluvial miasma that identified all the ills that still pervaded the species. The best efforts of fifty years of Gifted influence had not ended these infirmities. Twylea's reporting that the vision of "perfect society" was regressing was borne out by the studies, both those performed by her people, and those of the commoner scientists.

These people were in decline, even as the work of Dr. O's group pushed the capabilities of the Gifted higher. Their problems had devolved into a race against time, the work to save these people. The seriousness of the stakes was exactly why this psychological study she'd been drafted into was so genius.

Eek, how piteous it would be to devolve from Gifted to commoner. Or even worse, to be crippled, a deviant, grotesque being, sub-common. She stifled a shudder, and wished for a strong breeze to freshen the city air. Almost on cue, the whoosh of a bank of urban ventilators kicked on, and a cool breeze carried with it the fragrances of clean linen and endorphins.

Ahead, two city blocks through the adaptive building towers, the city center park rested, like an Eden of green abundance. The circular softwalk around it was always filled with people, a perfect place to make her show of busting the vial and releasing the harpies.

Before she reached the park, at the next crossroad, commoners clotted the softwalk, gawking at some disturbance on the parallel roadway. She approached and the crowd parted, letting her pass. She didn't possess the arresting beauty of a Social, but she was still physically enhanced to a degree, and an impressive figure with clear dark skin and thick tresses of raven hair that she wore pulled back and tied. When she reached the curbed edge of the road, she found a vehicle accident, a cargo van stopped, and the burly unshaven man she assumed to be the driver. He knelt at the front of the vehicle, blubbering like someone insane.

"I didn't see her, I swear. She jumped out like a blur, faster'n the brakes could react!"

The "she" he referred to was Twylea, lying on her back on the pavement, partially under the van's front tracks.

The driver jerked when he saw Reginah. "I tried to stop,

mum! I was too damn slow." He waved his hairy hands in the air above Twylea's face, afraid to touch her, or check for vital signs. From where Reginah stood, she could see none of the telltale signatures of life—chest rising, pulse in her neck and wrist, movement in her irises. Reginah didn't need to touch her to know the Social was dead. Reginah's throat clamped tight, so she could barely swallow.

To those pressing in around her, she asked, "Anyone call this in?"

An older woman about a foot shorter than Reginah, with limp graying hair and a pre-cancerous growth on her sallow face, said, "Yes, mum. I've signaled the Corp, and they're comin'."

"Very good."

The others crowded tighter, violating Reginah's space, risking the wrath of her discomfort. Some twitched the micro-cameras in their fingertips, capturing the scene. The driver buried his face in his hands. "Why did she do that? Oh god, I'm soooo sorry!"

Reginah willed the Social to end this ruse and rise, but she remained still and dead, with blood leaking from her sculpted ears and the corners of her temptress lips, the lavender pool eyes blood-rimmed and clouding over. Reginah forced herself to look away and surveyed the crowd instead, most standing motionless and stunned. Several men and women stared at Twylea and fondled themselves, apparently overcome by her beauty, even in death. Reginah felt her disgust rising like vomit. She wanted to strike them.

A few in the crowd were not staring at the dead Social. To a person, they were leering at Reginah with a combination of hatred and lust.

The wail of the Corp response team insinuated itself into her senses. To the older woman, she instructed, "Stay here until they clear the scene. Make sure you impress to them that it was not the driver's fault."

Which it wasn't. The modern auto-braking systems were nearly perfect at preventing accidents, and also vehicular suicide. Unless the victim was extremely motivated and quick.

She gripped the vial tightly in the bottom of her tunic pocket, and then stepped into the street and kicked Twylea's body once, hard, in the ribs. She ignored the squeals and gasps of the onlookers and walked away, leaving the smell of them behind her. At least the fool driver was shocked out of his inane sobbing.

She melded back into the flowing mass on the softwalk, back in the direction of her office, away from the city center, away from the crowds.

A few steps from her building, an opalescent tower shaped like a piece from an elaborate board game held the escalator down to the first level of the Under-City, a cavern of shops and restaurants that evolved almost nightly to address the changing needs of the populace. She paused and let the flow of commoners pass her by, all of them giving her a wide berth, but glancing back in curiosity. Rationals did not pause; they acted with decisive correctness, as if their actions would change the course of the future.

She pulled the vial from her pocket and eyed it, and her logic center fed her the new probability that it was what Twylea had claimed, well over eighty percent. There were dozens of commoners taking the escalator downward. She could toss it here and walk away.

Instead, she flicked the end of the vial off with her thumb, exposing the contents to the air. She raised it slowly to her nose and inhaled deeply, smelling ethanol, amines, potassium salts, and proteins.

She pushed into the flow of people, smelling their infirmities again. As she descended, she tapped drops of the liquid onto the handrail, then at the bottom wafted the nearly empty bottle back and forth among the throng. A young mother with a bluebell hair scarf pushed a child carriage with year-old twins dressed in the horrifying colors of pink and baby blue. When the mother looked away at a direction sign, Reginah sprinkled drops of liquid over the children's heads. She abandoned the empty bottle in a trash de-constructor.

She walked among the shops then, finding what she needed, a small auto-pay store that was serving as an apothecary by day. It would transform into a social club for dinner or recreational drug use in the evening. When she entered, faces turned toward her, like the dishes of radio receivers. There was one worker or proprietor, a man of perhaps 50 years, with a clear bronze face and ebony hair too nice, enhanced in the lesser ways available to a commoner with good finances. Surprised and uncomfortable, he watched her as she searched among the aisles, until she found the place where deodorants were displayed. Across the aisle, feminine cosmetics were arranged in colorful rainbow displays intended to hook the users. When she stopped there, examining the products, the man approached.

"G'day, ma'am. Is there something I may... assist you with?"

She gestured toward the cosmetic display. Her fingers

were long and straight and sublimely shaped, and her nails perfectly symmetrical, without a cuticle. They would not remain that way.

"I'm," she said. "I'm... going to need... some of these things."

* * *

This story first appeared in the After Dinner Conversation—March 2022 issue.

Discussion Questions

1. Was it ethical to enhance 2% of the population in the first place, if the entire population was not able to be enhanced?

2. Does the human race have a collective obligation to continue to improve our species? Does the human race have any collective obligation at all?

3. It is okay for those with enhancements to have greater influence over the course of the world? Should the smartest make the policy decisions for the world? Is there a group that should have a greater world influence? Is there a group that currently does?

4. According to the reading, enhancing the 98% will wreck the 2%. Would anyone in the 2% ever volunteer to give up their place of distinction? If you were in the 2%, would you?

5. It is ever ethical to take away from one person, to raise up another? What about our progressive tax system that taxes the rich at a higher rate to benefit those with less? Can you think of other "real world" examples that you agree or disagree with?

* * *

The Empathery

Hannah Baumgardt

* * *

Content Disclosure: Sexual Innuendo

* * *

Losi came home from school with a body from the Empathery.

Carol stood in the kitchen making lasagna. The garage door slammed, and she wiped a strand of hair off her forehead with the back of her wrist. She listened to her children kicking off their shoes, then their hissing whispers. Carol straightened from her cooking, leaning the heels of her palms against the counter's edge.

"You two had better not be planning anything," she warned.

The whispers quieted. Someone called, "Hi Mom."

"Losi?" Carol leaned over the counter to peer down the empty hall leading from the family room to the garage. The voice didn't sound like Losi—too low, too nasal—but the rhythm of the words was the same. Carol waited for her two teenagers to waltz around the corner, but the hall remained empty.

"It's me, Mom." Losi's strange voice drifted over the walls. "I got an assignment at school today."

It was probably a cold. Something had been going around school lately, and Losi must have caught it. Carol returned to layering noodles and sauce in the glass dish. "This had better not be a complaint, missy. Homework is a requisite part of education."

"We know, Mom," Cole droned, and Carol closed her eyes and shook her head.

Losi said, "My English class was talking about empathy..."

Carol's hands went limp over the lasagna. Dread settled like a crouching tiger in her stomach. She had to swallow twice before she called, "Losi, if we're going to have a conversation, I want to see your face. When you talk to someone, you look them in the eye."

They were familiar words, something her husband told the kids every time he lectured them. Carol clung to the phrase, drawing composure from it. She listened to the shuffle of feet down the carpeted hall.

Losi stepped into the kitchen. Blonde hair coiled in a braid over her shoulder and down her chest, where her hands fiddled with its end. Blue eyes flitted about the room, wide and worried. A wine-spill birthmark splashed her jaw and leaked onto her neck. The dread began to lash its tail, and Carol leaned against the counter and folded her arms over her chest to contain it. This was not Losi. Losi had Dave's dark hair and Carol's green-brown eyes. But as she waited for Carol to say something, the girl's foot tipped onto its toe and rocked back and forth—one of Losi's nervous habits since childhood.

"Losi!" Carol snapped, pleased the ring of authority hadn't fled her voice.

"It was a school assignment, Mom," the girl said in Losi's words, though not her voice.

Cole edged into the family room beside his sister. Carol felt her insides go limp with relief at his familiar whip-thin form topped by hair swept with too much gel. He was two years younger than his sister, but had already passed her in height. The blonde in the family room stood even with him. Some detached part of Carol wondered if that pleased Losi.

"Your teachers should know better," the more present part of her said. "It's a fad—technological trash. Worse than plastic surgery—and you know my rules about that." She let Losi wither under her disapproval for a few seconds. "How long do you keep it for?"

"Just two days, Mom." The girl's foot rocked back and forth, twisting at the knee.

"Just two days." The tiger in Carol's stomach paced circles. She flung down the towel she'd used to wipe her hands and returned to the lasagna.

* * *

Carol passed those two days in an unease she could barely explain to herself, much less express to Losi. She grew tense and fractious, anticipating relief that never came. Losi got her body back from the Empathery on the third day, certainly. But that night, Cole came home as a pudgy redhead. He tried to sneak up the stairs, but Carol heard him knock into the kitchen's side table, no longer familiar with where his body ended. Her porcelain vase shattered on the tiles and a strange voice began cursing.

Carol set her knitting down on the bedcovers and came to stand in the doorway between her bedroom and the family room. She watched her unfamiliar child sweep the shards into the dustpan. Her throat burned, though whether with tears or anger she could not tell. She felt as if she were watching a thief break into her home, but instead of jewelry or electronics, he stole her children's bodies, removing any sign of familiarity.

"Cole?"

He covered his face with an arm. The motion tugged up his shirt, revealing a sliver of pale, fat waist. "Mom..."

"Is this for class?" she demanded.

"Gym."

"Gym? Gym! What use does Mr. Cobb have for the Empathery?" Kids had enough insecurity in their *own* body without dealing with a second.

The boy dumped her vase into the trash. "It's supposed to make us want to exercise more. It's stupid!" His face had flushed bright, matching the tomato of his shirt. "I hate it!"

Sharp satisfaction needled Carol's chest. "Good. Maybe you'll learn empathy." She had meant the words to be an ironic reference to Cole's arguments over the past two days, but they came out flat. Before he could read anything into them, she added, "Two days?"

Cole nodded, not meeting her eyes.

* * *

On the fifth day, her husband's coworker Khyl came home for dinner.

"Well, hello, Khyl!" Carol said, her eyes darting about the family room to make sure nothing was too out of order. "Dave invited you to supper? I've got—"

"Honey, it's me," Khyl said. He crossed the family room into the kitchen, sweeping her into a hug.

"Khyl!" She struggled against his embrace.

The man stepped back. "Carol, I'm sorry. It's Dave. It's me." He gestured up and down the stocky body.

"Dave?" Her voice sounded accusatory, though she hadn't meant it to be.

"It's a team-building exercise for work." Khyl-Dave shrugged. "The boss is friends with the empath, so it's probably more of an advertisement. But I'm certainly not complaining." He flexed, biceps pressing against his plaid work shirt. Then he leaned in, grinning. "And tonight, you won't be either."

He wiggled his eyebrows ridiculously—the expression she most loved on Dave's face, the sort of humor she had fallen in love with him for. On Khyl, it nauseated her. She pushed him away. "Khy-Dave. Honey." She turned her back and breathed. The man stood behind her, an unfamiliar shadow. After a moment, she heard him retreat. Dave always knew when enough was enough, but the new weight of him made the floorboards creak an unknown tune.

Carol slept with a strange man that night. They lay on opposite sides of the bed. This had always been Carol's favorite moment of the day, with Dave all to herself, his arm over her side, their fingers entwined. Tonight, she lay on her back with arms folded over her chest. Something about that muscled body beside her made Carol feel old. Dave had taken the hint, and the small space between them filled with their silent alertness.

In the darkness, Carol asked the question that had been eating her all evening.

"Dave? Does someone have your body?"

He stirred beside her, air whistling through his nose as he breathed in. "Well, yes. It's an exchange."

She had suspected, but horror still rose to choke her. Had the children also exchanged? What had her family's bodies done without them? "Khyl has it... you... your body?"

A rough hand settled on her forearm, the same gentle touch, but so different from Dave's hand. She flinched away, and the hand withdrew.

"Is that a problem, Carol?"

Carol said nothing. She tilted her head to stare at the green glow of the bedside clock. Eleven. She wondered what time Khyl and Elaine went to bed. Elaine was so young—thin and beautiful.

In sudden spite, Carol said, "Kiss me, Dave."

He hesitated a moment. She didn't move as he leaned toward her, but tilted her head to meet his lips. They were fuller than Dave's, and the fringe of beard tickled her jaw. His hand moved to cup her cheek. The fingers were shorter and didn't tickle at her ear as Dave's would have.

The kiss didn't last long. Dave drew back, his breath warm against her chin as he tried to find her eyes in the darkness. The covers rustled as he rolled back to his side of the bed.

Carol pressed a finger against her lips, feeling her heartbeat. Her want to somehow hurt Elaine washed away in a rush of shame and regret. She hadn't kissed another man in years. Tears slipped from her eyes as she blinked, trickling past her ear and onto the pillow. Was she unfaithful for wanting to? Lustful for taking pleasure in those lips?

As if sensing her pain, Dave said, "Carol, it's just a body. It doesn't matter." His voice sleeked into sarcasm. "After all, you fell in love with me solely for my irresistible charm and wit." She could hear Dave's smile under Khyl's voice.

Carol licked her lips to cool them, wiping her cheeks. That was true enough, wasn't it? She would love him no matter what body he had. He didn't doubt that, did he? But it was hours before she slept, and when she did, she dreamt of Dave and Elaine.

* * *

By Saturday, everyone was back in their correct bodies. The return didn't provide the relief Carol had anticipated, however.

"I thought it was okay. I learned a lot," Losi said over dinner. She had braided her dark hair in a thick plait over her shoulder and was twitching its end. Losi had never worn her hair like that before; the blonde had.

"I hated it." Cole smudged mashed potatoes over his plate. He'd penned himself in his room for most of his two days and tried faking a cold to get out of school.

"You just got cheated. Next time, you can pick a better body."

"Next time?" Carol demanded.

Losi glanced at her. "Well, I mean, if we ever do it again." Seeing Carol's expression, she added, "It wasn't so bad, Mom. You should try it."

Carol opened her mouth to snap something she would probably regret, but Dave laid a hand on her forearm and squeezed gently. He moved his hand down to hers, entwining their fingers. "Don't worry, Carol. It's not as bad as you think. It's important to understand where others are coming from, and this is a better way than any I've heard of. We all learned good lessons."

He raised his eyebrows at Losi and Cole. Losi nodded with innocent eyes. Cole shrugged and grumbled, stabbing at his broccoli.

Carol resisted the urge to demand what lesson her husband had learned. That he liked those muscles? That he would start working out now? That his wife was a prude? Instead she snapped, "The empath is an immoral, commercialized fraud. He doesn't want to teach anyone empathy. He just wants to get rich." Dave rubbed the back of her hand with his thumb, fine-boned and long. She took a breath, calming herself. "There's no empathy—it's just a body. Your mind doesn't change." Her voice sounded so firm, so sure.

"Even if it is only bodies, I still think it's cool. And teaches you a lot," Losi added. "Maybe I'd choose a boy, next time." A teasing smile quirked her mouth. "I bet I'd learn even more."

Dave barked a laugh.

Carol pushed back from the table, sweeping into the kitchen to start the dishes.

* * *

Despite Carol's best efforts and sternest looks, the conversation continued in snippets and references for the next two weeks. She asked Dave to drop it, thinking *he* could have some self-control if the kids didn't. He never brought the Empathery up to her face after that, but the experience hung behind his eyes, in the silence that fell when she entered a room.

The first week, Carol was angry and annoyed. Losi and Cole, she could understand. They were young—children, really. But Dave? She had spent more than half her life with him. Now she couldn't see him without thinking of that unfamiliar body breathing beside her in the bed. Was Elaine thinking of Dave? Carol's own, beautiful Dave?

The second week, she realized Dave's experience with the Empathery had changed his life. He would talk about it for years, though never to her. It would haunt his dreams and become the stuff of daytime fantasies. He would look at her with eyes doubtful, curious. Would he prefer her as another? Would she prefer him as another? Those two days would lie forever twitching between them, unacknowledged, unforgotten. A slowly rotting corpse with half-recognized features.

So when Dave suggested the family spend a weekend at Cedar Lake, Carol told him to take the kids. She could use some time alone to finish the blanket she was knitting for their newest nephew.

She waited a full four hours after the Subaru pulled out of the driveway before starting the sedan and heading into town. The drive only took five minutes, but it felt like fifteen, and Carol nearly turned back three times. In the parking lot, she braced herself against the seat with hands pressed to the wheel. She stared at the flowing blue letters on the brick building. *The Empathery*. She took a breath, then unbuckled and exited the car in one motion, as if jumping into icy water.

A string of bells chimed against the glass. Carol stood on the mat as the door swung shut behind her. The room was small and bare. Its white walls were pocked by frames. Most displayed reviews or newspaper articles, though the two largest hung behind the white marble counter along the left wall, bearing the golden seals of diplomas.

"Hello! What can I do for you?"

A man slid from a door behind the counter and came to

fold his hands over the marble. He was bald but for a few wisps combed over the top of his head, and his nose was large enough that the rest of his face seemed to shrink from it. He noticed her examination and smiled. His upper lip was thinner than the bottom, though both shone fleshy pink. Carol didn't return the smile.

"May I presume you are here about a body change?" the empath said.

His crisp manner made Carol chill. She stepped up to the counter, mirroring his demeanor. She was vaguely pleased to find that if she straightened, she stood a good deal taller than the empath. "Yes."

"Wonderful. And would you be wanting a fitting or simply an exchange?"

Carol's eyes flickered away and back to the empath. "I'm not familiar with those terms."

"Certainly." The man smoothed the lapels of his white lab coat. "During an exchange, you pick out a body which has been left by another. You might recognize the person. Anyone else purchasing an exchange today would then be able to choose your body."

Carol struggled to maintain her neutral expression.

"A fitting is more private. I have a number of donated bodies available for my clients. You can choose from a selection of over twenty, and I will keep your body here until you are finished."

He smiled. Carol wanted to spit in one of his smug, glassy eyes.

"How much does each cost?"

"Five hundred for an exchange, one grand for a fitting."

Her face slackened. "One grand."

"Yes, ma'am. It's a new and growing business. Once the technology is more widely available, cost will go down, of course. But right now, there are only two places in the world offering my services, and you're in one of them. Believe me, the price will be worth it when you tell your grandchildren you were among the first to use an Empathery!"

So much money. Of course, neither the kids nor Dave would have had to pay that. They probably got a considerable discount, even a free trial. They were walking advertisements. She forced herself not to think of Losi and Cole in an exchange. What their bodies had done beyond their control, beyond Carol's discipline...

She almost left then. A fitting was beyond her means and the thought of someone masquerading in her body made her feel ill. But she saw herself standing with Dave, a rotting corpse vaguely reminiscent of Khyl lodged between them, straining any contact, any conversation. She would not lose Dave so easily. Carol put one hand in her purse, counting by feel her roll of cash. Her credit card would have covered it, but she refused to put the charge on a bill for Dave to see.

Carol stared at the empath and his sticky smile, hating him for what he had done to Dave, what he was making her do. She spread her cash across the marble. "I'll take an exchange, then."

* * *

Carol examined the strange woman in her closet's full-length mirror. She was at least ten years younger than Carol, with legs smooth to the point of glossiness. Carol had rubbed those legs together during the ride home, amazed at the taut slip of skin over skin, backed by toned muscle beneath. Carol lifted onto her toes before the mirror, regretting she had never invested in heels. A pair of calves like that needed to be shown off.

She scowled suddenly, dropping back to the carpet. Vanity hadn't plagued her since she'd turned forty. Carol glared at the woman in the mirror, but couldn't maintain the expression. She twisted up an eyebrow, then frowned, then bared her teeth. Each movement felt so familiar, all her muscles sliding into line, but on that strange face... Was this what her expressions looked like to Dave? Was her glare really that severe? Or did it just look worse on this woman's makeup-glamoured face? Carol raked amber hair back from the forehead, looking for any trace of familiarity on the strange visage. Nothing.

Panic spiraled through her chest, tightening around her lungs. She felt the horror of a hundred spiders creeping over her frozen body. She wanted to run from the mirror, peel her skin off like latex and find herself beneath, throw herself to the ground and thrash and roll... Instead, she laughed an unfamiliar laugh, high and manic, and stared at the strange blue eyes wild with her entrapment.

Her five hundred dollars gave her a day to enjoy the new body, as the empath had phrased it. Carol barely lasted that long. Her breath ran short the whole time, her head dizzy with panting. She didn't leave the house. She pulled the curtains, ashamed of anyone seeing her. This was the worst sort of delusion. She could fool herself with past beauty by wearing old dresses—the one she had worn at her sister's wedding, another for Cole's baptism—but in this body it was all too easy to believe she was something she was not. And through it, realize what time had really made of her. *No*, not her. Only her body. Only the body.

She didn't sleep. She sat in the family room, knitting with fingers suddenly clumsy, rubbing her perfect calves together. The only thing which kept her from crawling back to the Empathery was the possibility that her body wouldn't be returned yet, and she would die of panic on the sterile white tile of the reception room.

She thought of Dave, reminding herself why she was enduring this torture. But her mind kept asking if he would prefer this body. If he came home now and found her sitting there, would he be happier at her attempt to understand him and fix the rift between them or to see the beautiful new body? The thought drove her mad, and she shivered at the feel of another woman's tears sliding down her cheeks. She flinched at each sound, dreading the slam of the garage door. He wouldn't be back for another day, she reminded herself—he would never find her like this. She would never have to know what emotions crossed his face as he saw her. Why couldn't she stop seeing them, then? Desire, the sudden regret of realizing this was only for a day...

So Carol wept, and knit, her fingers dropping stitches, and cursed herself for her doubts and the empath for his temptations and Dave for desires she had perhaps only imagined in him.

* * *

Carol was parked in the Empathery's lot an hour before it opened, but she made herself wait five full minutes after the empath flipped his sign from 'closed' to 'open.' She refused to go sniveling to him, begging for her own body. Only after she had collected as much of her scattered mind as she could did she snap the car door shut and march inside.

"Ah, Mrs. Olerson. You're here to return the body?"

"Yes." Each breath reminded her of the terrible, beautiful form she wore.

"Your body was returned last night just before closing. If you'll follow me to the exchange room, we can get you settled back in." The man gave her a sappy smile and moved out from behind the counter.

Carol followed him through the door to the back room. The space was plush and dim, with red wallpaper and carpet that seemed Victorian in its luxury and romance.

"I—it—was used then?" She hated herself for asking, but panic squeezed the words from her.

"Of course, Mrs. Olerson. It's unusual for any of my bodies to go unrented."

But it had been returned last night. She could have come back for it. Why returned so early? Had the renter lost their nerve? Or was her body not satisfactory? She pressed her lips together and said nothing as the empath turned on a heel to face her and made a floppy gesture intended to be dramatic. Her body sat on a velvet chair in one of many glass tubes lining the wall. The eyes were closed, hands folded on the lap. The chest rose and fell in mechanical rhythm. The cheeks seemed to glow a youthful pink Carol hadn't seen on herself in years. In the room's dim light, the body looked alive and peaceful, not needing Carol and her worry and scowls to drag it down.

The empath took her arm and guided her to the chair in the center of the room. She shivered under the lidded glares of all the slowly breathing bodies in their glass cylinders.

"I'll have you sit here. Just so, very good."

He lowered the chair's visor, making her only one more sightless, breathing figure. She felt him attaching the little suctions and wires all over the body—palms, wrists, the balls of the feet, the perfect calves, as well as places under her clothes. This body blushed more easily than her own, and Carol felt the flush spreading down her neck. She was glad of the visor hiding her face.

"Very good. I'm going to hook you up to your body and you'll be back home in a flash. Just relax, now."

Carol breathed deep. She pictured Dave's grin, imagined sharing her experience with him, his arms around her as he realized the sacrifice she'd made. The space between them closed, knit together with love and understanding. Gone was the half-seen figure, decaying, unacknowledged.

"Ready?" came the empath's voice. "Three, two, one..."

* * *

Carol waited at the dining table. Dave and the kids would be home any minute now. She rubbed her calves together. They felt deflated, limp muscles sliding in wrinkled sleeves of skin. She forced herself to stop.

The garage door slammed open, and the bustle of voices and feet tumbled down the hall.

"I did not!" Cole said. "It was a perfect dive. It would've won a competition."

"In your dreams," Losi said. "I bet your stomach's still red from all the belly flops you did."

Dave's laugh rolled through the air to her. Carol pressed her palms against the table, sitting straight. Her husband came into the family room, smiling wide as he saw her waiting. "Home, honey!"

Carol stood and went to him. She smiled, but the expression felt forced. Was this how she always smiled? How could she not remember?

Dave bent to kiss her. She hesitated the barest moment before pressing her lips to his. Something about the kiss felt different. She stepped back, uneasy. What had changed? She almost laughed at the question. What had changed? She had lived a day in the body of a diva. Her own form had frolicked for hours untended by her mind, her morality. Dave had become Khyl, and she had slept with him. Dave's body had slept with Khyl's slip of a wife.

Carol opened her mouth to tell him what she had done for him, to close the space between them, but couldn't find the words. She felt her mouth hanging half-open, her eyes darting between Dave's. His expression grew concerned.

"Carol, did something happen while I was gone?"

She knew what he was asking, even if he hadn't fully realized it yet. Why had she stayed home? Why had her smile for him changed? What had she been doing while he was away?

"No, nothing," she said. It was the perfect truth to his deeper question. She had done nothing to hurt him. But her strained answer only deepened his confusion. She could see it like a bruise around his eyes.

"Dave, nothing. I only rented a body from the Empathery."

The bruise cleared. "You did? Carol, that's wonderful! I wish I would have been here. Maybe we could have enjoyed ourselves." He bounced his eyebrows, goading her for a response.

She knew what to do, and a week or even a day ago it would have come naturally. Now she had to prompt herself to laugh and shove him away. She pushed harder than necessary, and the terrible space opened between them, waiting to be filled, grasping for a form.

He didn't mean what he said. He was joking, that was what Dave did. She had fallen in love with him for that. But what had he fallen in love with her for? Carol rubbed her calves together, wondering, doubting. The space hung before her and she could see the figure lying there, blocking her way to Dave, blocking her truly seeing him. The figure's face was indistinct. It was Khyl, then a blonde with a wine-spill birthmark, then a round-cheeked redhead, then herself—no—only the body she had worn, only the body. But how could she know who was beneath? How could she see through the flesh, the rotting, shifting flesh? Could you separate them, the body and the mind? Could you know what made up the one you loved?

She was still floundering for words when he leaned in to kiss her cheek. "I want to hear all about it when I finish unpacking the car, right? You don't seem yourself."

"Who else would I be?" she asked Dave's back as he turned down the hall. Perhaps they would talk, and perhaps the space between them would fade. But she would never un-see that indistinct form, flickering, morphing, never stop wondering if Dave could see it too.

* * *

This story first appeared in the After Dinner Conversation—October 2022 issue.

Discussion Questions

1. If the technology in the story were real, would you be willing to try on a new body for a day? If so, what kind of body would you choose, and what would be your purpose in doing it?
2. Various people in the story argue that trying on a new body encourages greater empathy for others? Do you agree? If so, do you think learning this empathy by temporarily using a body should be required?
3. Do you think it would have been appropriate for Carol and Dave to make love while Dave was in a new body? What rules might you put in place for someone using a body?
4. What do you think is the underlying reason for the distance between Carol and Dave after the body exchanges?
5. If the technology in the story were real, would you be willing to try the body of a different gender? A different race? A different sexual orientation? With a physical disability? Is there a type of body you absolutely would not try?

* * *

Cost of Human Life

Shannon Frances Smith

* * *

Content Disclosure: Death or Bereavement

* * *

Donald Smith got up at his usual time of six in the morning to go to work. He tossed on a plaid dress shirt and jeans, the programmer's unofficial uniform. Getting his keys for his late model car and his wallet, he walked out the sliding door of his one-bedroom condo.

He was part of a development team at Canal Railroads. They were creating an AI to control the trains and rail switches. The AI's purpose was to automate the trains' running by making decisions usually made by an operator or engineer. The AI was in its testing phase, and on this day, Donald was tasked to put it to the ultimate challenge: The Trolley Problem.

The Trolley Problem refers to an exercise in ethics that goes like this: you have a runaway trolley going towards five people. The trolley can be diverted away, but the other track has one person on it. The trolley does not have time to stop for either. Do you divert the train?

This test was necessary for this very scenario could happen with actual trains. The algorithm had to do the right thing based on the information that had been fed into it. The AI's results doing the wrong thing would be the possible death of many and the loss of millions of dollars from train damage and lawsuits.

Donald got to his work station at the usual time to punch in the parameters. The desk itself was black with a white plastic surface where his computer tower and two monitors were sitting with a black swivel chair waiting for him. He saw various others from his team typing away at their stations, monitoring one thing or creating a change list for the other. A few business-dressed people walked by and exchanged words he did not understand before walking towards the breakroom.

Into the terminal he entered the data: five persons on a track near Kirby with a switch and control. The track ahead had one person on the diverted route. He punched in that the weather was a sunny day about twenty degrees Celsius, the track ran through a field and there was no damage to the rails. He also put in that it was noon on a typical Wednesday. These details might seem a bit much, but the model asked them as part of its decision making.

He waited for the result. In live production, this data would already be known or sensed by the AI. He entered the mock data and waited with a smug grin. "This is easy," he thought. "Kill one to save five."

Being a software engineer, he thought morality was an easy equation and debates on ethics gave him little interest. He was the product of an education that pushed STEM so hard things like critical thinking or ethics went by the wayside. He figured the computer would do the utilitarian thing to save the most lives without thinking about it.

His mind was blown by the AI result: do nothing, kill the five. Flabbergasted, he checked the debugging console. The console reported no errors; the algorithm ran as expected. It went through all the epochs, and everything in the neural network weighted it. *Why not divert the train?* He thought as he then looked into the log file the AI generated to see what it found.

"Diverting the train creates a ~35-minute delay and inconveniences several hundred passengers on the waiting stations and on the train itself. While the one person should not have been on the track, the family of the struck person can also sue and collect ~$100,000 as diverting the train caused their death, when no action would have kept them alive." The log read, "Cost to clean viscera ~$1500. Cost of waiving fares for train delay fault with Canal Railroads ~$2000."

"What about the five that died on the tracks?" Donald asked rhetorically, "Can their families sue for the lack of action?"

He kept reading: "The train going about its normal operating sequence would go through this path. As the train was operating normally and the five should not have been there in the first place, Canal Railroad cannot be held responsible for their deaths. ~ $0 collected from them. ~0 minutes delay would occur. Cost to clean viscera: ~$3000. No fares waived as five humans will not create enough resistance to delay the train." The truth of the last bit stung as trains can plow through semis and still keep going.

Donald banged his head against his desk. "Is that the value

of human life? Less than a lawsuit and being a nuisance?" He looked at the log again and then looked into the code and the fed information from the training and test sets. He looked over the model and its pipeline with wild intent, scoring the lines of semicolons and braces, weird variable names and constants. The layers that made up the model's neural networks were under a lot of scrutiny. He looked at each variable tensor within the model, and the constants fitted in, desperate to assume he made a mistake and fed it the wrong data. How was each node weighted and layered?

He went into the breakroom to get a coffee. The coffee machine took his input, ground the beans, and sprayed the coffee into a waiting paper cup. Donald took the cup and added some cream and sugar, then sipped it. He had a moment where he thought, *"What if the information fed to the model was different? What if I changed the data points, and in turn, where the train was geographically and in time?"*

He went back to his station to rerun the model, setting the junction to one near Peterborough with the weather being a snowy negative ten degrees Celsius. The time and day were assigned to a typical Sunday at ten am. The rest of the information was the same. Donald ran the model with bated breath. After some time and sips of coffee, the results were disappointing: "Do nothing, kill the five."

Donald looked at it again. To do something: "Diverting the train creates a ~65-minute delay and inconveniences several hundred passengers on the waiting stations and on the train itself. While the one person should not have been on track, the struck person's family can also sue and collect ~$100,000 as diverting the train caused their death, when no action would have kept them alive. Cost to clean viscera ~$1500. Cost of waiving fares for train delay fault with Canal Railroads ~$1500."

To do nothing: "The train going about its normal operating sequence would go through this path. As the train was operating normally and the five should not have been there in the first place, Canal Railroad cannot be held responsible for their deaths. ~$0 collected from them. ~0 minutes delay would occur. Cost to clean viscera: ~$3000. No fares waived as five humans will not create enough resistance to delay the train."

Donald slumped in his chair, defeated. The one sticking point was that active action killed one person while doing nothing killed five, and it was arguably not the railway's fault if someone died from their inaction, but there was fault if their action killed someone. The one-hundred-thousand-dollar suit for the death of an ordinary person was what would ultimately weigh on the model's decision making. Having this functionality of this model realized didn't sit well with Donald.

In truth, there was no parameter for the value of human life, so the AI went with how either action would affect Canal Railroad monetarily, by design from the inception of the model. The meetings went into many ways for this model to value things, and no one argued when it was designed to value money. Most assumed that people had some monetary value—Canal Railroads can be sued for harming, maiming or killing one, or many in situations like a train derailment. Even in freight, human life was supposed to have a dollar value as some freight, like crude oil mixed with benzene derailing in the middle of a city, could cost enough in monetary loss to bankrupt Canal Railway. Money also was supposed to play a factor in things like train delays. Like many train services, fares got paid back in the event of a train delay, and fines were paid if said delays made freight late.

The least damaging result measured in time and money was to do nothing.

Donald left work that night with a bitter taste in his mouth after completing his crash course into ethics. He pondered the big lesson he learned while waiting in a traffic jam during rush hour, realizing that there was more to humans and human life than money, after all. However, a very uncomfortable question still crept into his mind that he couldn't quite beat back: exactly how much was a human life worth?

* * *

This story first appeared in the After Dinner Conversation—June 2021 issue.

Discussion Questions

1. The AI program has made the most cost-efficient choice: to do nothing and allow the five to die. Should cost be the only factor when making operating decisions of this type? What, if any, other factors should be taken into consideration?

2. They say you can't put a price on life, but juries do this all the time. The accidentally severed arm of a professional pitcher is worth more in a civil lawsuit than that of a normal person. Should there be a punitive damages cap in death cases? Is there a safe and effective medical procedure simply too expensive to offer to all citizens? Where, if anywhere, would you put price limits on life?

3. If you were the one controlling the railroad switch, would you pull the lever saving five people, and killing one? What is your reasoning? Would you be willing to harvest organs from one healthy person to save five other people? What, if anything, is the difference?

4. What, if any, changes would you make to the AI decision parameters in this story and why?

5. Does it matter that ignoring the cost of choices would mean higher ticket prices for everyone to offset litigation costs? What if a change in the AI to ignore choice costs increased train tickets by 10%, 50%, 200%?

* *

Author Information

Abrama's End Game

David Shultz writes fiction and poetry from Toronto, ON, where he runs the "Toronto Science Fiction and Fantasy Writers" group, and is lead editor at *tdotSpec*. He is greatly appreciative of his readers, including his 6,000 followers on Wattpad. David holds degrees in cognitive science, philosophy, law, and education. X (Twitter) *@DavidFShultz*

The Formula

Richard Shury studied literature at Otago University, and is a sci-fi nerd. Successes include his piece Chiaroscuro read at Liars' League, while the short stories Ricky's Journey and Gamer have both been published in anthologies. He hopes these are the calm before a storm. Call him a part-time optimist. *@RichardShury*

Give The Robot The Impossible Job

Michael Rook is a Washington, D.C.-based author and member of the Horror Writers Association. His short story "The Gangsta Confirmation" recently appeared in Buckshot Magazine, while other short stories such as "The Boxer" and "The Rails" have appeared in horror magazines and anthologies. Currently, he's completing his first novel, a supernatural horror tale about a strange horse ranch. He also enjoys sci-fi and thrillers. Instagram *@michaelrook10*

Sow

Joseph Bodie is a writer living and working in San Francisco, where he received his Masters in Writing from the University of San Francisco. His work has been published in such journals as The Tishman Review, Newfound, and SLAB. He is currently working on a collection of experimental short stories.

Cicada

Ishan Dylan is a conservation biologist and fiction writer from the Chesapeake area. His work is forthcoming in *Exposition Review's* 'Lines' issue. X (Twitter) *@IshanDylan*; *www.ishandylan.com*

The Things We Give

Allison Padron is an M.A. in Writing student at Rowan University. She lives in New Jersey with her husband and her three cats, Basil, Sushi, and Tofu. In her free time, she enjoys reading, knitting, and visiting national parks. Twitter *@apadronwriting*; *www.allisonpadron.com*

Two-Percenters

CJ Erick stumbled into Dallas in search of love, great sushi, and access to big box stores. Having found all three, he now inhabits the city with his wife and their two ponderous and entertaining black-and-tan hounds. When exhausted from the reckless adventure of engineering, he pens tales of the space frontier, gothic horror, the occasional steampunk mystery, and other unbalanced visions from caffeine-deranged nightmares.

The Empathery

Hannah Baumgardt lives in Minnesota, working as a stained-glass designer and dreaming of owning a dragon. But she would settle for a dog, too. You can find her work at Daily Science Fiction.

Cost of Human Life

Jared Cappel's prose has appeared or is set to appear in various publications including Idle Ink, Literally Stories, and City. River. Tree. When he's not writing, he enjoys creating digital art known for its abstract imagery and vibrant use of color. A lover of wordplay, he's ranked as one of the top 50 Scrabble players in North America. *fineartamerica.com/profiles/jared-cappel*

Additional Titles

After Dinner Conversation - *Technology Ethics*

After Dinner Conversation - *Crimes & Punishments*

After Dinner Conversation - *Bioethics*

After Dinner Conversation - *Nature of Reality*

After Dinner Conversation - *Equality Ethics*

After Dinner Conversation - *Research Ethics*

After Dinner Conversation - *Government Ethics*

After Dinner Conversation - *Business Ethics*

After Dinner Conversation - *Examining the Past*

After Dinner Conversation - *Food Ethics*

After Dinner Conversation - *Sex & Sexuality Ethics*

After Dinner Conversation - *Interpersonal Ethics*

After Dinner Conversation - *Interpersonal Ethics*

After Dinner Conversation - *Philosophy of Religion*

Or subscribe to our monthly print/digital magazine.
www.afterdinnerconversation.com

Additional Information

Reviews

If you enjoyed reading these stories, please consider doing an online review. It's only a few seconds of your time, but it is very important in continuing the series. Good reviews mean higher rankings. Higher rankings mean more sales and a greater ability to release stories.

Print Books

https://www.afterdinnerconversation.com

Purchase our growing collection of print anthologies, "Best of," and themed print book collections. Available from our website, online bookstores, and by order from your local bookstore.

Podcast Discussions/Audiobooks

https://www.afterdinnerconversation.com/podcastlinks

Listen to our podcast discussions and audiobooks of After Dinner Conversation short stories on Apple, Spotify, or wherever podcasts are played. Or, if you prefer, watch the podcasts on our YouTube channel or download the .mp3 file directly from our website.

Patreon

https://www.patreon.com/afterdinnerconversation

Get early access to short stories and ad-free podcasts. New supporters also get a free digital copy of the anthology *After Dinner Conversation–Season One*. Support us on Patreon!

Book Clubs/Classrooms

https://www.afterdinnerconversation.com/book-club-downloads

After Dinner Conversation supports book clubs! Receive free short stories for your book club to read and discuss!

Social

Connect with us on Facebook, YouTube, Instagram, Bluesky, TikTok, Substack, Meetup.com, and X (Twitter).